W9-BFO-881

NINE MONTHS

Luciana

by Maggie Wells

E
EPIC
Press

Luciana
Nine Months: Book #6

Written by Maggie Wells

Copyright © 2016 by Abdo Consulting Group, Inc.

Published by EPIC Press™
PO Box 398166
Minneapolis, MN 55439

Printed in the United States of America.

Cover design by Candice Keimig
Images for cover art obtained from iStockPhoto.com
Edited by Lisa Owens

LIBRARY OF CONGRESS CATALOGING-IN-PUBLICATION DATA

Wells, Maggie.
Luciana / Maggie Wells.
p. cm. — (Nine months ; #6)
Summary: Luci wants to be a celebrity and she'll do anything to make that so. But
when she finds out that she is pregnant she has to face her father and the dark family
secret that he's been hiding. Ultimately, Luciana wants a clean break from her past—
so she decides to abort the baby. Will she ever be at peace with her decision or can
she overcome the regret and loss she feels and get on with her life?
ISBN 978-1-68076-195-5 (hardcover)
1. Teenagers—Sexual behavior—Fiction. 2. Teenage pregnancy—Fiction.
3. Sex—Fiction. 4. Abortion—Fiction. 5. Young adult fiction. I. Title.
[Fic]—dc23
2015949415

EPICPRESS.COM

In memory of my mom

One

"**H**I, IT'S ME, LUCI," I SAID INTO THE CAMERA. "WELCOME to my fucked up life." I had been posting videos on Facebook and YouTube since I got my first iPhone at age ten. Of course my parents had no idea what I was doing. They barely knew how to use the Internet, for God's sake.

"Let me ask you a question," I said into the camera. "Does your dad call you names? Because mine does. Moon-monster is what he calls me." I stepped back from the tripod so that my audience could get a full-body shot. "I look normal, right? Now, anyway. But unfortunately I was freakishly tall in elementary school. You know—always told to stand in the back row for classroom photos, holiday concerts and the like." I sat back down in front of the camera. "Moon-monster—can you imagine? Do you know what that does to a girl's self-image? He even sings it to me. Ever heard the song 'Moon River'? I'll sing it for you: 'moon monster, taller than a mile . . .'"

I turned the camera off and saved the file to my hard drive. "Let's tag this one 'Poor Body Image,'" I said out loud. I posted it to YouTube along with an instrumental soundtrack of "Moon River."

That video got seven hundred views.

//

But I showed my dad—I got my revenge. Because when I turned fourteen this year, off came the braces and in came the boobs. I grew my hair out and bleached it blonde and all of a sudden boys began to notice me. Even high school boys started to notice me. Popular girls who I had assumed did not even know my name suddenly invited me to join them at their lunch table. I was one of them—I was a *popular*!

Okay. I knew the boys called me *Luci-balloons* behind my back and I could feel their eyes staring at my chest. But you know what? I didn't care. At least I wasn't invisible anymore. I was getting invited to parties for the first time in my life. High school parties!

"Hi, it's me again," I said into the camera.

My life was pretty pathetic. While other girls were playing soccer or field hockey after school, I sat alone in my bedroom and made YouTube videos hoping to build a following. And I was willing to do pretty much anything to achieve that. Because here is the thing—the thing I would rather die than say on camera or even write in my diary—is that I wanted to be rich and famous. I hated being middle class, ordinary. I wanted to be a star, wear fancy clothes and jewelry every day. I wanted to be Kim Kardashian.

"So I was at this party last night," I said into the camera. "And after a few shots, I was dancing on the table and someone shouts out for me to show my tits. Now girls, let's face facts. To have the attention of boys is the most powerful feeling on earth. When a boy wants a girl, he is relentless. I can feel the tug of his orbit from yards away, his stare burning my skin like a heat lamp. And it triggers something in my brain—serotonin, I think they call it. It's like a drug. I would do anything to get the attention of a boy. So sure, I show them my tits. And then some boy tells me how beautiful I am and offers to drive me home from the party. And asks me to touch his penis." I paused for dramatic effect.

"The penis is an insane body part. It has the air of hopefulness, coupled with something that almost borders on pleading: 'Please stroke me! I am nice!'

"Penises to me are a lot like puppies. Detached from the boy that it belongs to, it is soft and appreciative and responsive. It's easy to get its attention and even easier to train it—to get what you want from it. So sure, I have sex. I have lots of sex with anybody on the basketball team or the baseball team or the tennis team or the swim team. But not the football team. Those guys are brutes and can't be trusted not to drug your drink and gang-rape you. Believe me—it has happened to more than one girl at my school."

I played back that section of the video several times to amuse myself. *Penises are like puppies.* I giggled. *That will be the title of the video!* I turned the camera back on.

"As a fourteen-year old, I have pretty much unlimited opportunities to have sex. And what I really love about sex—it's getting the whole attention of another person all to myself. For the only time since I was five and lay on the floor pretending to be dead and Mom hovered over my body, pretending to cry, I could have somebody else's attention all to myself. I think this is the real reason people have sex—to get to a place where there is nothing else but you and this other person who wants you. I never want it to end."

My first time was in the way back of Keith Campbell's father's station wagon. Keith was a popular senior. His little sister was mentally retarded—*what's the politically correct term for that? Challenged? Whatever!* I guess out of guilt, his parents gave Keith a very long leash and his was the go-to place for Friday night post-game parties. I looked directly into the camera.

"Keith—he was my first—he paid me a lot of attention and made me feel like I was the most beautiful girl in school. He told me I was special. That he couldn't believe he was with me. When he held me, I felt like a present all wrapped up with a shiny bow that he didn't want to share with anyone else. He said it was his first time, too. But his kisses got harder and harder. And his hands were everywhere at once. And then he was inside of me, thrusting and moaning. It hurt and I just held my breath waiting for him to finish.

"The second time we did it was at a party in someone's bedroom where all the coats were piled high on the bed. I listened to the party noises going on outside the door, people laughing and shouting. The bathroom door swinging open and slamming shut. Keith didn't even kiss me goodbye when he was done. I wiped my eyes and sat on the edge of the bed trying to remember the words he had said. How he had filled me up, filled the aching hole inside of me, made me feel whole and alive. But how when he pushed himself inside of me, suddenly I was empty again. I usually felt like crying after it was over. He would finish and sometimes, I would have tears rolling down my cheeks and he would hold me. But that didn't make me feel any better.

"Then there was the time we did it in the bushes in the yard outside the house where the party was going on. I don't really remember much about that time. I heard about it in school the following Monday.

"You would think I would eventually wise up to his lies. A boy will say anything to get what he wants from a girl: 'You're so hot. I have to have you. If you loved me, you would.'

"Each time I thought, this is it; Keith really loves me. His hands felt so good, wanting me, needing me. His words made me feel beautiful, irresistible—even powerful. If I gave him what he wanted he would stay with me forever. I felt enormously useful. Keith needed to come and I made that happen. I had a simple purpose.

"But of course, everything changed once we had started having sex. All of a sudden the hours we had spent talking and making out were gone. The time he spent with me seemed rushed and frantic. He no longer took me anywhere except to some deserted place to be alone. Sometimes we would stay in the car outside the party. Sometimes we would get a blanket and spread it on the grass.

And then we would have sex, and it would be over in a few minutes. It was always hurried and almost rough. Having sex had taken me to a completely different world."

I turned the camera off. I thought back on how it had ended. Keith came over on my birthday and handed me a little flowering cactus in a pot. A cactus!

"Happy Birthday," he said.

I felt terrible. I hadn't gotten him anything for his birthday.

"Here's the thing, Luci," he said. "I really like you and all, but I'm not in love. I don't think we should see each other anymore."

I know what you're thinking. Oh my God, she must have been crushed. But actually I didn't feel anything at all.

"Okay," I said.

I think that hurt his feelings.

That video got seven thousand views.

Two

"**H**i, it's me again," I said into the camera. "So my parents are getting a divorce. I know what you're thinking: join the club, am I right?"

"So my mom is always angry—in a violent kind of way. Like the time she threw a glass of milk at me and then had to take me to the emergency room to get stitches. In my face! Just because I said I didn't like sweet potatoes, or maybe it was mushrooms, I can't remember. Maybe she gave me a concussion—I can barely remember the incident at all. I always wondered how she explained my facial wounds to the ER doctor."

My mom was a roadside IED just waiting to

be tripped over. I was so afraid of setting her off on some irrational tirade. Once she had poured her first cocktail of the evening, I had to tiptoe around the house to avoid any kind of interaction with her.

"I think my mom hates being a mother—or being a wife—or maybe both. She had a couple of nervous breakdowns when I was little. That is what my dad called them. I suspect they were actually suicide attempts. Before she checked herself into the hospital each time, I remember coming home from school and how everything was silent and dark in the house. I thought no one was home but then I remembered that my mom's car was in the driveway. So I looked around the house and I finally found her upstairs in bed. She had the covers pulled up to her chin and she was just lying there, staring. She looked at me and it seemed to take her a few minutes to recognize me. She said she wasn't feeling well. I thought maybe if I left her alone she'd feel better later.

"There was this one time when she collapsed in the front hall, sobbing hysterically, just before the ambulance arrived. Dad glared at me cowering on the stairs. 'Look what you've done to your mother!' he yelled at me. I don't know what he meant by that. Except that I guess that my very existence served to make my mom want to off herself?

"When she left us, she was usually gone for a week and every time when she came back, she was a different person. Her eyes looked funny and dazed all the time. I wondered if they had locked up my real mom and sent someone else to our home."

I paused the camera and stared off into the distance. *Wow, my parents are getting a divorce. What is going to happen to me?* I turned the camera back on.

"When my dad comes home from work every day, he goes straight to bed and takes a nap. I have to wake him up for dinner. And then he barely talks at dinner. In fact, I don't remember my parents ever really fighting. But tension inhabits our house like an unwelcome guest that nobody wants to offend by telling him the party is over and it's time to go home."

I paused the camera again and grabbed my journal to jot that down—*like an unwelcome guest—I should be a writer!* I turned the camera back on.

"Mom is a screamer but Dad refuses to ever raise his voice. And Mom really hates that about him. His passive response just makes her angrier. I think she actually hit him with a frying pan one time. At least that's what he said. Maybe he was joking, I don't know. Sometimes I wake up in the middle of the night and hear them talking in low, sharp tones. Then my stomach starts to hurt so I bury my head in my pillow to drown them out and try hard to fall back to sleep.

"This morning," I said to the camera, "Dad came down to breakfast with a big bruise on his nose. He said mom had bit him. So he's moving out and taking me with him. To Cedar Rapids, Iowa, can you fucking believe it?"

I turned off the camera. I filed that video under "Domestic Violence."

That video got nine hundred views.

//

I was off-line for a week while my dad and I packed up and moved. Cedar Rapids turned out to be my worst nightmare; the place was so sleepy that freight trains ran right through the middle of downtown and cars lined up on either side of the barriers for fifteen minutes or so, several times a day. Dad claimed he loved the small town life, but then again, he had grown up on a farm in Wisconsin. What does he know?

We were living in what had once been a church rectory but had since been converted into apartments. Our apartment was on the first floor, which used to be the chapel. The living room had a weird raised platform in the middle where the altar once stood. Dad thought it gave the place, quote, *character*. I thought it was quote, *stupid,* as it made it impossible to arrange the furniture in any normal formation. And there was the issue of navigation in the dark when I had to get up to pee at night. My knees were scraped and scabbed from tripping over that damn platform.

The best thing about the place was the hammock in the back yard. Dad had strung this cool old hammock up between two trees. The hammock was my refuge—the place where I would go and think my thoughts.

"Hi, it's me," I said into the camera. "Welcome to my hammock." I zoomed the camera out to show me lounging in my hammock. "Here we are in Cedar-fucking-Rapids." The cicadas made loud chirping noises in the background.

"Luciana!" Dad yelled from the kitchen window. "Get up out of that damn hammock and come help me make dinner."

"And that's my dad," I said. "He doesn't like me lying around all day while he is at work. And I don't, really. Not every day. Sometimes I ride my bike down to the high school and shoot video of myself practicing my serve on the deserted tennis courts. Two cans of neon green balls, six serves, then walk around the net to gather them up and serve again. Those were pretty boring videos. I didn't bother to post them on YouTube."

"Once in a while other people show up to play on an adjacent court and one time this guy calls out to me: 'You're always here—don't you have anyone to play with?' So I look at him. He was kind of cute and I suddenly felt embarrassed. Discovered by a cute guy while hitting tennis balls all by myself on a sunny Wednesday afternoon in June? So I don't answer him. I didn't think that kind of question deserved an answer—right? What's wrong with practicing your serve? I could be a famous tennis teen sequestered in Cedar Rapids to perfect my technique away from the throngs with their video cameras. I wish I had said that to him—but I didn't think of it until later. It came to me while I was lying in the hammock. I read somewhere that Serena Williams's dad made her practice her serve for six hours every day.

"Anyway, I better go see what my dad wants." I turned off the camera.

//

"I got you a job," Dad said into the camera.

"What kind of a job?"

"Would you turn that off!" he said.

I turned off my phone and put it in my pocket.

"My boss, Mr. Rupczynski, needs a sitter for his kids this summer. His daughter is visiting from Indiana and his new wife has two sons, seven and eight. Roxanne is your age, fourteen."

Roxanne Rupczynski! I thought. *What an unfortunate name.* "Why can't Roxanne babysit?"

"She's a bit immature," Dad said. "On the spectrum, as they say."

"Autistic?" I asked. "Is she going to punch me?" You never know about these autistic kids; there was a boy in my sixth grade class who got suspended three times for hitting teachers.

"She's not going to punch you," Dad said. "But the boys won't obey her. I lied and said you were fifteen."

"You did?" *Dad lied about my age?* I looked at him with renewed admiration.

Three

ROXANNE WAS SKINNY AND GANGLY WITH BUCKTEETH AND a harsh Midwestern twang that made her sound like an ignorant hick. I swore I would never go to Indiana if that's the way they talked there. Her stepbrothers, Mike and Artie, on the other hand, were compact and cute. It was sad. *How would you feel if your dad's new step-kids were that much cuter than you?*

Roxanne's dad never said anything to me about Roxanne being autistic. It seemed like it was a family secret or something—like it was something he was hoping his new wife wouldn't notice. But she knew, obviously! Because while the boys weren't allowed to watch TV or play video games, Roxanne was the only one who was allowed to use her computer.

What do you do to entertain kids in the summer in Iowa? This was my challenge. In order to alleviate boredom and keep myself entertained, I created a new YouTube channel called *LuciSitsinABox* and began a daily vlog of my baby-sitting experience at the Rupczynski's house.

Mike and Artie were perfect subjects. The boys were funny and full of energy so every morning we rode bikes to the park to play catch and hit tennis balls. I would follow them around all day with my iPhone camera set on video mode and ask silly questions for which they offered even sillier answers.

Me: "Why are trees tall?"

Artie, with a quizzical look: "How tall are the trees on the planet that you are from?"

Me: "How small are the people on YouTube?"

Mike, pinching his fingers together and squinting into the camera: "This big."

That video got three thousand views.

//

I filmed the boys playing tennis, a game in which every other ball was hit over the back fence. Every afternoon we went to the community pool, where I filmed them splashing around and jumping off the diving board.

Mike: "When do we learn how to breathe underwater?"

That video got thirty-two hundred views.

//

Roxanne wore a tiny string bikini. I thought about filming her as she sashayed around the deck, trying to draw attention to herself but that felt a little exploitative. So, while the boys took their swimming and diving lessons, Roxanne and I sunned ourselves on striped towels that we spread out on the steaming concrete. I was working on an awesome tan—one that I could not wait to show off to all the boys back home in Pittsburgh, assuming I could ever go home again.

On rainy days, I played Yahtzee and Go Fish with the boys and taught them how to play chopsticks on the upright piano in the upstairs hall. I don't know why the piano was in the hall. That's the thing about babysitting—the parents are entrusting you with not only their precious little darlings, but also the intimacy of their quirks and habits.

Roxanne was always glued to her computer. If her father knew what she was doing on her computer, I am sure he would have banned it as well. But I wasn't going to tell him that she had posted a profile on OKCupid or that she was chatting with men, some as old as thirty!

"I have a boyfriend," Roxanne said into the

camera. "His name is Isaac and he said he wants to meet you."

"Me?" I asked. "Why would he want to meet me?"

"He asked me about you and I told him you were really pretty," she said.

"Well, that's kind of creepy," I said.

"Can he come over?" Roxanne asked.

"Have you met this guy?" I asked. "I mean in person?"

"Last Saturday," Roxanne said. "Dad dropped me at the mall and Isaac met me there."

"What did you do?" I asked.

"We had sex," Roxanne said.

"At the mall?" I asked.

"No!" Roxanne laughed. "Sex at the mall—how does that even work? No, he took me to his house."

"Roxanne, that sounds really dangerous," I said.

"Sex?" Roxanne asked. "I love sex. I have sex all the time, back home."

That video got one million views.

At this point, I paused the camera. "Does your mom know?" I asked.

"No," Roxanne said. "And don't you tell her!"

"I don't even know your mom," I said. "How could I tell her anything? How old is this dude, anyway?"

"Isaac?" Roxanne asked. "He's twenty. Do you want to meet him?"

"No, I said. "And I don't think you should be seeing him, either."

"Have you had sex?" Roxanne asked.

I know what you're thinking. I was the babysitter, paid the big bucks to protect my young charges. But her question took me by surprise. Should I pretend that I was a virgin to set an example for her? That might make her seem more experienced than me—that could adversely affect our sitter-sat relationship. On the other hand, would admitting that I too "loved sex"—and for probably all the same reasons that she did—be seen as encouraging her risky behavior? Let's face it—I didn't give a shit what she did with boys on her own time. She certainly wouldn't be having any sex on my watch. I decided to deflect the question.

"Roxanne," I said. "Sex is a very private thing. It's not something you go around talking about. Have you ever heard your dad talk about it? Or your mom or your teachers? That's just something that adults do not do. You are very mature for your age and you should start acting like a grown-up, right?" Okay, so I was laying it on a bit thick. But she took the bait.

"You think I am mature?" she asked.

"Yes," I said. "You have the body of a woman."

Roxanne grinned and embraced me in a big hug. "Isaac tells me that I am beautiful," she said.

I heard their words in my head: "You're so beautiful."

"Roxanne," I said, speaking slowly. "Boys will

say anything to you to get into your pants. Anything. Let's face it, boys lie."

"You don't think I'm beautiful?" she asked.

Okay, now we were getting into some dangerous territory.

"Give yourself a few years, and I think you have all the signs of growing into a real beauty someday," I lied. I don't even know where I came up with a stupid phrase like that. With those buckteeth she would be more likely to grow up looking like a horse.

Four

UNBEKNOWNST TO ME, ROXANNE HAD TOLD ISAAC TO meet us at the pool the next day. While the boys were in the middle of their swimming lessons, Isaac showed up. He was a tall, wiry, black dude. He stripped off his t-shirt to display his ripped abs and pecs.

Roxanne jumped up. "Isaac!" she squealed. "You came! Do you want to go in the pool with me?"

I sat there helplessly as Roxanne jumped into the shallow end and Isaac followed. I watched them frolicking and tackling each other, splashing everyone around them. I had no idea how her bikini bottom managed to cling to her bony ass as she dove after Isaac. But I filmed every second of the action.

That video only got five-hundred-thousand views.

//

Clearly, Roxanne hasn't thought this through. How is she going to keep the boys from telling their mom?

Finally they got out of the pool. Roxanne scooted self-consciously into the restroom and Isaac approached our spot on the deck.

"Isaac," I hissed. "Do you see those little kids in the red trunks?" I gestured toward Artie and Mike.

Isaac nodded.

"Those guys are Roxanne's brothers—well, step-brothers, actually," I said. "They could get you two busted. I need you to pretend that you two just met. You just met at the pool, right?"

"I'm cool," Isaac said. "You'll tell Roxy?"

"I'll handle her," I said. "When the boys finish

their lesson, we'll introduce you as someone we just met, and then I think you need to go sit somewhere else. On the other side of the pool or something."

"That's okay," he said. "I know when I'm not wanted. I'll take off. Let Roxy know?"

"Even better idea," I said.

///

"Where's Isaac?" Roxanne cried when she emerged from the restroom.

"He said something about work," I lied. "Where does he work?"

"Some burger joint downtown," Roxanne said. "He is a cook."

"Well, there must have been some fast-food emergency," I said. "He had to take off."

"I'll text him." Roxanne dug in her tote bag for her phone.

Shit! I forgot to clear the story with him. What if she catches me in a lie?

She emptied her tote bag on the pool deck. No phone. "Damn!" she cried. Fortunately, she had left her phone at home.

"Want me to text him?" I suggested. "What's his number?"

She actually knew his number by heart.

I texted Isaac: I told Roxanne that you had to go to work. Cool?

He responded, OK.

"I told him you left your phone at home and you'll text him later," I said. "He said okay."

She stood there, gangly in her skimpy bikini, squinting off into the distance as though she might see him lurking behind the fence or something.

"Why don't you practice your underwater swimming and when the boys are done, we'll go home and I'll make a snack?" I suggested.

"All right," she said with a big sigh.

I had just gotten out of the water and was lying in the sun to dry when a shadow loomed over me.

"Hi," the shadow spoke.

I shielded my eyes and squinted up. I looked around for Roxanne. She was in the pool, doing awkward handstands in the shallow end. *Where is my camera when I need it?*

"Mind if I sit next to you?" he asked. He proceeded to spread his towel out on the deck and the edges of his towel encroached slightly onto mine. He was wearing a faded blue speedo, which was snug against his junk, and nothing else. I sat up on my elbows and bent my right knee, doing my best to look fetching.

"I'm Chip," he said. "You are here every day."

I looked at him harder and recognized him. Chip was one of the lifeguards, as well as the boys' diving instructor. His chest was covered with curly hair that had been bleached blonde from hours in the punishing sun. His torso was toned a deep bronze and his nose was covered in a thick layer of zinc oxide.

"Mike and Artie, right?" he asked. "Are they your brothers?"

"I am the babysitter," I said.

"You're the babysitter? Wish I had a hot chick like you sitting me when I was seven! Do you have a name, babysitter?" he asked.

"Luci," I said. I had been admiring Chip from afar for weeks, his stocky, muscular torso that he had honed as captain of his high school diving team. I particularly liked filming him as he walked around the deck of the pool, his gaze always fixed on the kids in the water. I loved the way he strutted around the pool; I suspected he knew that all the girls were staring at the curve of his ass, which threatened to burst the seams of the tired old nylon. Most of the day he sat in a deck chair in front of the pool office, his eyes behind dark lenses fixed on the surface of the pool. But every so often, the guards would shift positions and then he would climb the ladder to the guard chair that was bolted to a platform suspended high above the deep end. From there he would yell at the kids to stop horsing around on the diving boards.

"Aren't you supposed to be saving lives?" I asked.

"I'm on a break," he said. He lay down on his back. "Out late last night, need a nap." His voice faded. "Wake me up in fifteen minutes?"

I lay down close to Chip and inhaled his scent of coconut oil, perspiration, and zinc oxide. I set the alarm on my phone for fifteen minutes and closed my eyes. I figured the other lifeguards could keep their eyes on Roxanne and the boys.

The alarm jolted us both awake.

"Ugh," he groaned. "Back to work." He leapt to his feet athletically and rolled up his towel. "What are you doing Friday night?"

"Me?" I asked.

"Want to go to a party?" he asked.

"Sure!" I said. "Can you pick me up from babysitting? Like six-thirty?"

Oh my God! The hot lifeguard that I have been lusting over for weeks just asked me out! This could turn out to be the best summer ever!

Five

O N FRIDAY EVENING, I WAITED AT THE CURB IN FRONT of the Rupczynski house wondering if Chip had forgotten about inviting me. Or maybe he hadn't really meant it. I was about to get on my bike and head for home when he pulled up in a cherry-red pickup.

"Sorry I'm late, kid," he said. "I had to close the pool tonight." He picked up my bike with one arm and lifted it into the bed of his truck.

I climbed into the passenger seat and Chip hopped in behind the wheel.

"The party doesn't start until nine," Chip said.

"I thought we could go down to the river and hang out. Do you want some?"

Chip took a hit on a joint and offered it to me. "Sure," I said.

We drove to a secluded spot in a wooded area. Chip turned off the engine and sat staring through the windshield into the distance.

My phone buzzed. It was a text from Dad.

Where are you?

I told you I was going to a party. Home by 12.

Your curfew is at 11.

OK, Dad. 11!

We're leaving early tomorrow for Batavia.

I know!

"Who is that?" Chip asked.

"My dad," I said. "My aunt died."

"Do you need to go?" Chip said.

"Her funeral is tomorrow," I said. "In Illinois. He wants me home by eleven o'clock."

"No problem," Chip said.

Chip took my hand and we walked along the Sac and Fox trail, dodging horse riders, bikers, and joggers. Can you believe it? I was actually thinking about Rox and the boys—wondering if I could bring them here—a little diversion from our usual routine of park and pool.

"This is really nice," I said.

"There is a little place up here," he said. He led me to a spot a little bit off of the trail, a patch of grass that was surrounded by brush and hidden from the path.

"Let's sit down," he said.

He spread out a blanket and offered me a flask.

"Thirsty?" he asked.

I took the flask and sniffed.

"Vodka?" I asked.

"Yes," he said. "Do you like vodka?"

"Who doesn't?" I said. I took a big gulp. The burning in my throat quickly became a sensation of warmth that spread down through my neck and shoulders.

Chip grinned in approval.

He pushed me down onto the blanket and pressed his body onto mine. He still smelled like the pool. He held me down with all of his weight and pressed his lips to mine. I melted into him.

With one hand, he pulled a sheet out of his backpack and spread it over us. There really wasn't much in the way of foreplay. He took off my clothes and then he took off his clothes. He offered me some weed. I said okay. He offered me some more vodka. I sipped it and kind of liked it. He offered me some pills. That seemed a little scary, so I told him no, thanks. Then he buried his face in between my legs. I couldn't figure out what I was supposed to do. He lapped at me like a dog at his water bowl. It was not that it was unpleasant, exactly, but frankly, I got a little bored. *Okay,* I thought. *I hope this is doing something for you, because it's not doing anything for me.*

At some point he decided that he was ready or I was ready or something. He made me get on top of him and all I could think of was that scene in Lolita. Yes, I read literature!

///

I woke up shivering, naked under the sheet. The stars were out. Chip was passed out next to me, snoring gently.

I pulled my clothes on quietly. He hadn't moved so I poked Chip on the shoulder. He moaned.

"Psst," I hissed. "Wake up!"

Chip came to and pulled his pants on.

"What time is it?" he asked.

I checked my phone. "Nine-thirty," I said.

"Do you still want to go to the party?" Chip asked.

"Okay," I said. "But, remember I need to be home by eleven."

"Right," Chip said.

We walked back to his truck. I fixed my makeup in the rearview mirror.

"That was my first time," I lied. I always said that, although the boys back home didn't seem to believe me anymore. I assumed that word had spread.

"Geez," Chip said. "How old are you?"

"Fourteen," I said.

"Geez," Chip said again. "It sure seemed like you knew what you were doing."

//

The party was loud. A crowd of drunken college kids played beer pong in the dining room, shouting over the music blaring from the sound system, while others smoked pot in the backyard. I went off in search of the bathroom and when I returned, Chip had disappeared. I perched on the arm of the sofa and considered my alternatives. I whipped out my iPhone and started filming the party. It wasn't long before some dude approached with an extra cup in his hand.

"I've been looking for you everywhere," he said, oblivious to the camera.

"Do I know you?" I asked. I accepted the plastic cup and sniffed. "What is this?"

"It's called a boilermaker," he said. "Taste it. It's good."

I took a tentative sip. It tasted bitter. What did he take me for, a fool? I'd heard all the stories of girls being drugged at parties. I made obvious glances over his shoulder.

"Are you looking for someone?" he asked. As soon as he turned his head I dumped the contents of the cup into the crack between the sofa cushions.

He turned his attention back to me and leaned over me. His breath was hot and acrid. His sweat smelled like day-old beer. He grabbed my breasts and clawed at my buttons.

"Hey, take it easy," I cried. "Don't rip my blouse."

"I bet you got great tits," he slurred. "Let me see."

I pushed him hard and he staggered backward.

"Bitch!" He lunged at me but I dodged away and he crashed into a floor lamp, knocking it over.

Some guy rushed over. "Hey, dude," he said. "Don't trash the place!"

That video got two million views. My audience was growing.

//

I took advantage of the chaos to escape to the front porch. Chip was sitting on a bench making out with some girl. His hands were inside her shirt.

"Chip," I said. "Can you give me a ride home?"

Chip looked up at me. His eyes were slits.

"Never mind," I said. "I'll call a cab."

//

Dad was already asleep and I tiptoed through the apartment, skirted the stupid raised platform, and crawled into bed.

Six

THE NEXT MORNING, I CHECKED THE CALENDAR ON MY phone and counted the days since I had entered an X indicating twenty-eight days. *Shit! My period is two weeks late!*

Dad was in the kitchen making breakfast. As soon as the smell of eggs and bacon wafted into the air, I had to rush to the bathroom. There wasn't much in my stomach to throw up. My mouth tasted sour afterwards and the smell of my own bile made me retch again. When there was nothing left inside of me, I splashed cold water onto my face and smothered myself in a washcloth. I brushed my teeth and stared into the mirror.

Damn it! I have to walk right past the kitchen to get to my room.

"Breakfast!" Dad yelled through the bathroom door. "Eat up and we can hit the road."

"I'm not hungry, Dad," I said weakly. I stood in the bathroom, afraid that if I opened the door the kitchen smell would overwhelm me and I would be sick again.

"Luciana!" Dad yelled. "Breakfast! Let's get a move on!"

"I'm not hungry!" I managed to yell this time.

I need to get a pregnancy test and find some place to take it. I could not imagine driving all the way to Batavia not knowing for certain. But then again, spending a whole weekend in the car with Dad and knowing that I was pregnant scared the shit out of me as well.

I know just what he'll say when he finds out: 'I'm not angry. I'm disappointed.' Of course not; he never gets angry. Not Dad.

But angry would be so much better.

Warm summer rain spattered the windshield and the wipers slapped, slapped, slapped, not quite in time to the country music on the radio.

"How far is it to Batavia?" I asked.

"About three and a half hours," Dad said.

"I need to stop at a drug store," I said. "Female stuff."

"Right now?" he asked. "Couldn't you have taken care of it yesterday?"

Yes, I could have, I thought. *But I didn't.*

"I guess I can wait until we get there," I said.

I stared out the window at the rolling fields of corn. Every few miles we passed a weathered farmhouse cradled in a grove of trees, the shady yard sprinkled with a few sheds, maybe a rusted-out truck and a dog or two. As the road undulated, mile after mile, I imagined riding my bike clear across Iowa, the road carrying me like a surfer on a wave. Then the sun came out and I rolled down my window. The July air, heavy with the smell of the rich black earth, blew my hair back from my face. I caught my reflection in the side mirror. I had my father's nose and chin, but otherwise my features were dark, not at all like his. He had clear blue eyes and sandy blonde hair. Since leaving Mom, he had taken to buying everything at garage sales: his furniture, even his shoes. On this day, he wore a threadbare sweater and baggy jeans that I feared he had dug out of some dumpster.

I trained my iPhone on him.

"You know, Dad," I said. "If you died in your apartment all alone, and your cat and dog were starving, your cat would eat you before your dog would."

"I guess that's why I have always been partial to dogs," Dad said.

That video only got five thousand views.

//

Eventually, we lost the signal on the radio and I had to scan the dial until we picked up a Caribbean station. Dad turned up the radio and beat the steering wheel in time, bouncing a little on the seat. I laughed and we sang along in a foreign language we didn't know.

After a while, static overpowered the signal and I couldn't find another station so I switched off the radio. I experimented with filming the farmland rushing by the car window.

"I need to tell you something," Dad said. "About your Aunt Sofia."

"What's that?" I asked idly.

"Well . . . she killed herself," he said.

I was shocked. I felt as though the world had suddenly tipped on its axis. *Sofia? The aunt whom I adored? Whom I had always wished had been my own mother?* Sofia was Dad's half-sister; Dad was the youngest boy in a family of eight and she had always doted on him. Aunt Sofia had six kids and her house was always filled with activity, joy, and laughter—so different than the vacant, sullen, accusatory atmosphere that I had grown up in. Everyone in Aunt Sofia's family actually seemed to like each other.

We had visited my cousins in Illinois every summer for as long as I could remember and I loved sleeping in the same bed with Sofia's daughters, Bonnie and Cindy. We would stay up all night playing truth or dare until Mom would come in and shush us. Never Aunt Sofia. She never scolded us. She was everyone's favorite aunt: so generous, always quick with a warm hug, a soft shoulder.

"What happened?" I asked.

"She walked into the river and drowned," Dad said.

"How can you just walk into a river?" I asked. The very idea terrified me—allowing the water to rush into your mouth and lungs, and fighting the urge to swim to the surface.

"It was about her mother," Dad said. "My mother—I never told you that she was murdered."

"You always told us that your parents had died of cancer," I protested. "Before I was born."

"It was easier to tell you that story," Dad said. "Who wants to tell his children that their grandfather had murdered their grandmother?" His voice took on a hard edge. "My father was a mean bastard."

I was shocked to hear the anger in his voice—I had never heard him use that word before.

"They fought all the time," he said. "He beat the shit out of all of us. And my brothers beat the shit out of each other—and me. Bastards! I hated them all."

It all started to make sense to me. Why my dad never raised his voice and never showed affection to my mother or me. What if you didn't know any other way to relate to your kids and your wife?

"What about your sisters?" I asked.

He grew quiet.

"When he was drunk and in one of his rages, he would drag one of the older girls upstairs and do only God knows what. Not Irene and Susie—they were too little. But all of us kids fled the farm as soon as we were of age. Flo ran away to Chicago when she was fourteen or fifteen, I think. Mom sent Sofia to live with her grandmother on the farm up in northern Wisconsin. I enrolled in NROTC and went off to college at seventeen."

We drove in silence for a long time.

"Ma left the farm once the kids were all gone," he said, suddenly. "She couldn't take it anymore. She moved back to Milwaukee. My dad was never much of a farmer—so he sold the cows and the farming equipment, and what was left for him to do? He sat through the winter in an empty farmhouse on an empty farm. I guess he decided to kill himself."

"But why kill your mom?" I asked. "How did that happen?"

"Somehow he got a note to her saying that he needed to see her," he said. "She stopped by the farm on her way to Sofia's house and he ambushed her. When Mom didn't show up, Sofia got worried and went looking for her. She found the bodies."

"The bodies?" I shrieked.

"He shot her and then turned the gun on himself," Dad said.

Just then, the clouds opened up and big drops slammed against the windshield and exploded like water balloons. I rolled up my window and Dad switched on the wipers.

"I don't think Sofia ever got over it—finding the bodies," he said. "She carried this secret like a stain," Dad said. "She never felt worthy of her husband. She walked into the Rock River and drowned herself—twenty years to the day after she found the bodies. The fourth of July."

Just then, I realized that my phone had been recording the whole time. Hoping Dad didn't notice, I closed the app.

Seven

SLUMPED DOWN IN THE SEAT, PRETENDING TO SLEEP. I HAD completely forgotten about my problem, becoming fixated on the memories of the times that Dad had taken us to visit the old farmhouse where he grew up. And now I started to question what was going through his mind each time we visited. The last time we were there, the house was empty and we were able to sneak in through the kitchen door and look around. The house was really spooky—the kitchen still had the original cast-iron stove and scarred linoleum floors. The light switch in the stairway was cracked and the wallpaper was scarred with scratches that looked they had been made by fingernails.

As the exit for Batavia approached, I said, "Drugstore, Dad. Please?"

Dad used the men's room while I rushed through the Walgreens checkout line with an EPT kit and a package of tampons, just in case. I took the test in the restroom, a weird place to do it, I know, but I thought taking it there would make it less likely to come out positive. I was wrong.

Of course I was pregnant. They tell you that condoms are eighty-two percent effective and diaphragms are eighty-eight percent effective and even that the pill is only ninety-one percent effective. Well I must have been that unlucky one percent, because my partners and I used all of those and yet, I found myself pregnant. And I had no fucking clue as to who the father might be.

As I stared at the plus sign, I felt completely powerless and saw absolutely no way out of this situation. I had never known another girl my age who had gotten pregnant so I couldn't think of anyone to call. Certainly not my mother and I didn't really have any friends in Cedar Rapids. I thought about my sweet Aunt Sofia and suddenly I realized that I was not sad that she had died. I was jealous. I wanted to be the one in the coffin with everyone crying over me.

I sat crumpled on the floor of a filthy toilet stall in a Walgreens in bum-fuck Illinois. The feelings of rage, shame, and guilt rose in my throat like sour bile. The muffled noises of customers outside the bathroom door washed over me as the events of the past six months played back in my mind, over and over, an endless loop, as I counted the rivets that marched in a line along the ceiling over my head. Each time I heard someone pound on the locked door, I jumped. But secretly, I was hoping for an explosion, a pressure-cooker bomb tossed by a rogue madman, which would shatter the plate glass and engulf the entire Walgreens in flames.

They would never find my scorched body, never be able to retrieve the fingerprints from the EPT stick that led to the perpetrator of the crime. I wanted the floor to open up and swallow me whole, along with my guilt and my shame. I turned the camera on myself.

"Hi, it's me," I said. "I just found out that I am pregnant." I turned the camera to focus on the plus sign on the stick and then back to my face, streaked with tears.

"I have no fucking clue who the father is. How fucked up is that? I don't know how to tell my parents and I can't even think why I should go on living; I feel so hopeless. I am such a failure!" I started to sob.

"I hate myself for being completely useless. Nobody loves me or wants me or needs me. I blame myself for believing all those boys who had told me they loved me. This is it. I am fourteen and pregnant and a total failure and a complete disappointment to my parents."

Dad was waiting impatiently by the car when I finally came out.

"What took you so long?" he asked. "Is everything okay?"

"Yeah, sure," I said. I climbed into the car and immediately put on my headphones so he wouldn't even attempt to make conversation with me.

//

Here's the thing about offing yourself. The people who are hurt the most are the ones who are left behind. I barely recognized my cousins when we arrived at the house. The boys were hanging out on the front porch, sprawled in the July heat on white wicker chairs. I sat down beside them, not knowing what to say. What I felt most was the silence—and I realized that I was the only one who was crying. Sofia, in ending her pain, created a lifetime of hurt for her kids and everyone else. This woman, who I had known to be so loving and giving, had taken everything from everyone. Having escaped the clutches of violence, she had created a happy family. And I believed that they had been truly happy. The happiest moments of my childhood were the times when I was embedded in her brood. Embedded and embraced. I felt love from that family that I never felt from my own. How had she maintained that façade of happiness for twenty years? And what made it come crashing down?

I looked around for answers. I looked at my cousins, numb in their silent misery. Their world had come to an end. The loss was unfathomable. I looked at my father. He had said all he was going to say.

"You look different," Cousin Jimmy said.

Cousin Jimmy had driven out to Pittsburgh to visit us the previous summer in a Vintage Pontiac that he had lovingly restored.

"In what way?" I asked, vamping a little. I had a big crush on Jimmy. Maybe he was seeing me in a new light?

"You look really pretty," he said. "Not that you weren't always pretty, I mean."

"Thanks," I said. "You look great, too." I wondered if we would end up kissing in the back hall of the funeral parlor. First cousins—that could be problematic—but then again his mom was only a half-sister to Dad. Does that make us half-cousins? Is that legal in Illinois? You can see how my mind works.

I thought about the stain. What was the nature of Sofia's stain? A secret so dark that she had buried it deep inside for fear that if someone else found out they would hate her and abandon her. Did my uncle hold it over her when they quarreled? Did he threaten her with exposure? How much did you have to hate yourself to off yourself like that? And now the stain had been passed onto her kids.

Doesn't that mean that my dad also carries the same stain? And then I realized that he did. The stain had poisoned our family too. The stain was shame. The crucible of violence in which Dad was raised had cast him as a leaden lump of passivity. He spent so much energy bottling up the aggression that he believed was inherent in his nature that he had long ago become unable to express any emotion at all. He had never once in his life hugged me or told me that he loved me; he never raised his voice or hand to me either. Whatever feelings he had for me he channeled into hurtful ridicule that he tried to laugh off as playful teasing.

Shame—I am intimately familiar with that feeling. I have felt shame for as long as I can remember—ugly, unlovable, a monster. So this is my legacy.

I started to think about Sofia differently. She had felt shame all of her life and when her husband came along and loved her and legitimized her, she felt validated and at the same time, she felt unworthy. Just like I had felt validated by the high school boys who were so eager to get inside my panties. And now the stain was in me.

I found a spot to perch on the railing to check my Facebook. On a whim, I searched on teen moms and found a page called Nine Months. There was a video posted by a chick named Jasmine.

Jasmine: "Can I Live" is based on a true story from Nick Cannon. Check out his music video . . .

I don't know what I was thinking but I posted a comment: Making a big life change is scary. But you know what's even scarier? Regret.

Candy: I'm 17 and I got accepted to Princeton. My parents don't know that I'm pregnant.

Aleecia: Where is the baby-daddy?

Candy: He's back in Italy with his family. He doesn't know.

Shawna: You gotta tell him, girl! He should step up.

Candy: I doubt it. He's already moved on. We haven't really talked since spring break.

Isabella: Tell your parents. Today. Let me know what happens.

I sent friend requests to all of the girls who had

posted on the page so they would follow me. Then I posted a link to my video shot in the toilet of the Walgreens: "Hi, it's me. I just found out that I'm pregnant."

That video got two million views.

Eight

FUNERALS ARE WEIRD—PEOPLE MILLING AROUND AND speaking in low voices. My Aunt Marie came up to me and told me not to cry. *Why shouldn't I cry? Isn't that what you do at funerals?*

I wanted to ask questions. Why had she done it? Had there been warning signs? Had my aunts and uncles talked about their parents' deaths over the years? Did Sofia's kids know about the murder?

My crazy Aunt Irene was there. She had never married, had spent some time as a nun, and then became a nurse.

"How old are you now, Luciana?" Aunt Irene asked.

"Fourteen," I said.

"And do you have a boyfriend?" she asked.

"No," I said. It wasn't a lie. I had been with lots of boys but none of them thought of me as their girlfriend. Of that, I was sure.

"Don't wait too long," Aunt Irene warned. "Look at me. I had a suitor once, when I was your age. My father drove him off with a shotgun and little did I know that would be my last chance in life. You need to get married."

It was such a surreal conversation. I was fourteen and pregnant, for Christ's sake!

After the funeral, Dad drove me out to the lake to visit my Aunt Flo, his oldest half-sister.

"You can stay at Flo's tonight," he said. "I am going to stay with Uncle John. He shouldn't be alone right now."

//

Flo was perched on her usual bar stool inside the dimly lit and musty pool hall. I climbed up onto a stool next to her. I loved hanging out with Aunt Flo. She smoked cigarettes and told dirty jokes. She was so cool, letting me sit in the bar with her and drink Shirley Temples.

"How come you weren't at the funeral?" I asked as I sipped through my straw. "Do you mind if I make a video?" I trained my camera on Aunt Flo.

"He killed her, you know," she said, slurring her words. She had obviously been in the bar all afternoon.

"Are you talking about my grandfather?" I asked.

"John," she replied.

"What do you mean—Uncle John killed her?" I asked.

"He never loved her," she said. "She felt worthless."

"She always seemed so happy, to me," I said.

Flo took a long drag on her cigarette. "He was sleeping with his secretary."

"Are you allowed to smoke in here?" I asked.

"How old are you?" she asked.

"Fourteen," I said.

"Is that right?" she said. "When I was fourteen, I ran away from home. Did your dad ever tell you that?"

"Where did you go?" I asked.

"I had to get away from that monster," she said. She didn't seem to be listening to me.

"Are you talking about your father? Dad told me he was a mean bastard," I said.

"He wasn't my father," Flo said. "My father died when I was ten. Then, when I found out that I was pregnant, I ran away."

"Me too!" I exclaimed.

"The nuns took him away from me," she said in between sips of her whiskey. "I never even saw my baby." She took another drag on her cigarette. "Wait. Did you say 'me too'?"

I paused the camera. "I think I'm pregnant," I said. "I mean I took a test and it was positive so I guess I am pregnant."

Flo put down her drink and looked at me hard.

"Were you raped?" she asked. "Does your father know about this?"

"No!" I cried. "And no, Dad doesn't know. Yet. Please don't tell him. I need to figure out what to do."

"Well, at least you can get an abortion," she said. "That wasn't an option for me."

"I would need parental consent," I said. "I would have to tell Dad. And probably Mom. Oh, God, she will never speak to me again."

"Your mom is kind of a bitch," Flo said. "She thinks she is too good for everyone else, especially your dad. She is just like your Uncle John. Too good for the rest of us."

"What should I do?" I asked.

"Who is the father?" she asked.

"I honestly don't know," I said. "Please, please, please don't tell Dad any of this."

"Well, isn't this a pickle?" she said. Aunt Flo put her arm around me. "You don't have to sleep with them you know. Just because a boy is nice to you."

I covered my face with my hands and dug my fingernails into my cheeks. I knew I was leaving welts. "You don't understand what it's like. How it feels," I said.

"I think I do," Aunt Flo said.

"I can't explain," I said. "It's just when I'm with them, I feel . . . like they care about me. They make me feel special, wanted—not just my body. But me, the real me. Like they could love me. But of course, I am always wrong. No one wants me. No one will ever love me."

"Flo," the bartender called out. "Your ride is here."

A cab was idling outside the front door.

"Thanks, Marco," Flo said. She downed her drink. "Come on Luci, let's continue this on the porch."

///

After her divorce, Aunt Flo had made the lake house her permanent residence. I made a video of the speedboats and water skiers racing by, leaving their wake to spill over the dock. Then I panned the camera around the room. The walls of the house were covered with framed photographs of Flo in her heyday. She had been quite a beauty and had spent some time in Hollywood as a young starlet. There were pictures of her with Arnold Schwarzenegger and other celebrities.

While Aunt Flo was busy in the kitchen I opened my Facebook app. Aleecia had gone to the abortion clinic and I needed to know what had happened next.

Aleecia: My momma said I can keep the baby.

Me: Did you go to Orlando?

Aleecia: Yeah, we drove up yesterday. There were protesters and everything.

Candy: I told my parents!

Isabella: And? Girl, don't keep us in suspense!

Candy: My mother is going to call her gyno to schedule an abortion.

Aleecia: They can't make you do that!

Me: I have to get an abortion. It's OK. I can't take

care of a baby. And besides, I don't even know who the father is.

Candy: I know. How am I supposed to have a baby and go to college?

Jasmine: People do it.

Aleecia: Kyle is going to college. We'll be OK.

///

Aunt Flo returned with a tumbler of bourbon and a glass of lemonade for me. She settled into a wicker rocker facing the lake view.

"When were you in California?" I asked.

"I told you that I ran away," she said. She looked at her drink.

That started me thinking. What if I ran away? Or what if I just stayed with Aunt Flo and never went back to Cedar Rapids or Pittsburgh?

"How far along are you?" she asked.

I stared at my hands with contempt, watching them twisting themselves into knots in my lap. To make them stop, I crossed my arms and buried my hands in my armpits.

"I don't want to talk about it," I said. "I just want it to be over. I—I want you to take me. Will you take me?"

"Of course, I will," Aunt Flo said. "But you have to tell your parents first."

I started to cry and buried my face in my hands.

"What will I tell them?" I asked.

"Just what you told me," Aunt Flo said. "And because of your age, we will need to establish paternity. You should make a list of every boy that you have been with—at least since March or April. You can't be more than a few weeks pregnant."

"What does my age have to do with it?" I asked, stupidly.

"You are fourteen," Aunt Flo said. "It's called statutory rape. The boy should go to jail. My step-father never went to jail. But he should have."

"Jail?" I cried. "No, no, no, no. That can't happen. I will never be able to show my face at school again. I won't be popular any more. Can't we just make this go away?"

Aunt Flo got up and came over to sit next to me on the loveseat. She put her arms around me and held me as though I were her own daughter. I sobbed into her shoulder, inhaling the scent of stale whiskey, cigarettes, and rose perfume.

Nine

HAD TO SIT AND WAIT FOR MY PUNISHMENT. I COULD HEAR Dad in the living room on the phone with Mom conferring. Dad's voice was low and calm, and Mom's occasionally audible, was peaking and plummeting.

I passed the time on Facebook.

Me: I just told my parents. They are fighting about it on the phone.

Jasmine: That sucks. We are here for you!

Aleecia: Kyle left for college.

Me: You will finish high school?

Aleecia: That is my plan. What's it like being pregnant in high school?

Isabella: You won't be the only one. You can form a club. An extra-curricular activity you can put on your resume!

Candy: Very funny!

Me: You can get a handicap permit.

Aleecia: I don't have a car.

Shawna: OMG! You'll ride your bike to school? Pregnant? Send selfies!

//

After an hour or so, Dad came into the kitchen, stood in front of me with his arms crossed against his chest, and laid down the law.

"Your mother and I have discussed it," he began, "and we have decided that you need to write down the name of every boy you have slept with this year. We'll order paternity tests on every one of them. And in the meantime, you will have to get an abortion."

I was watching his face, how it transformed

when he was angry. Like I said, Dad never raised his voice or shouted at me. But his face was distorted, looking all the more severe, the angles of his cheekbones hollowed out. He looked like a different person.

"How could this happen, Luciana?" he asked turning his face away from me. "How?" he said again, almost in a whisper. "You have always been such a good girl."

I heard their words in my head: "You are so beautiful."

"Aunt Flo said she would take me," I protested. "Can't she come with me?"

"That's nonsense," he said. "Flo lives four hours away—and she is never sober enough to drive. I will take you."

He tipped his face downward toward the sink. I bet he wished there were some dishes to do but he always made me wash the dishes as soon as I had cleared the table.

"Dad?" He still wouldn't turn around. "I'm sorry."

I waited for him to come to me and hold me and tell me that I would be okay. That I would always be his little girl. That he was sorry he let me go out to parties at night and didn't warn me about boys—that they would say anything. Even lie.

I waited for him to yell at me. To shake me and tell me what I fool I was. I waited for him to do something. Anything. *Please.*

But he stood by the sink with his back to me.

Not even my father could love me.

//

The waiting room was crowded when we got to the clinic. I tried not to look at the other women and girls waiting their turns. Only one of the girls was there with her boyfriend. They sat across from me, holding hands. The boyfriend rubbed his thumb back and forth across the top of the girl's hand in a calm, rhythmic way. She rested her head on his shoulder. He stared straight ahead. Dad was the only adult male in the room.

I checked out Facebook while I was waiting.

Aleecia: My baby daddy brought his little brother to come live with us.

Isabella: Who is us?

Aleecia: OMG! I forgot to tell you that Kyle moved in with me. We're living in my mom's garage.

Jasmine: You are living in the garage?

Aleecia: Kyle is a carpenter. He's putting in walls and everything. We live in Florida, so it's not like it ever gets that cold.

Me: So what's with the little brother? How old?

Aleecia: Dwayne is eight. Kyle's mom's boyfriend threw the boys out of the house. Can you believe that?

Shawna: I believe it. My mom is threatening to throw me out!

Candace: Jesus. And I thought my mom was a bitch!

///

They called my name and in a trance, I followed the nurse through the inner door. I didn't look back at Dad. The nurse was speaking in a weird monotone—like she was reading from a teleprompter.

"Here is the locker room," the nurse said. "Over there is the waiting room. Inside the locker room you will find a locker for your clothes. The locker does not lock. Do not leave any valuables there. Inside the locker you will find a paper gown and slippers. Put on the gown and slippers and wait in the waiting room for your name to be called. Do not bring anything into the waiting room with you."

This is a lot of information to absorb, I thought. *What if I get it wrong?* "What do I do with my purse?" I asked.

"What's that? What do you do with your valuables? You should never bring valuables to the clinic."

Well, wait. That doesn't make any sense!

"Here is your intake form. Fill this out and bring it with you to the waiting room. Check off the procedure that you are having. The procedure that you are having is called Manual Vacuum Aspiration or you can just tick the box for Medical Abortion. Tick a box for General or Local Anesthesia. The clinic does not offer General Anesthesia."

So, why is there a box for it?

She stopped and looked at me. "Do you need to collect a tissue sample to establish paternity?"

I nodded.

"Tick that off on the form too."

She turned and continued walking and pointing, pointing and walking. I followed her, numb inside.

"When you get to the waiting room, hand your form to the receptionist. She is a temp and she may not know what to do with it. The ladies room is over there. If you need to use the restroom, take your intake form with you. Do not leave anything in the waiting room. Just find a seat and wait for your name to be called. If your name is not called, do not ask the receptionist. She will have no clue why your name has not been called. Just sit and wait for your name to be called."

"When your name is called, follow Nurse Regina into the procedure room. The procedure rooms are to the left. Nurse Regina has an eight-year old son, Jacob, who she calls her miracle baby because he was born after her previous abortion was botched and left her scarred for life. Doctor Gellhorn will be performing your procedure. Doctor Gellhorn is in love with Nurse Regina. He talks dirty to her while he is performing procedures. She finds it mildly amusing. Jacob is not his son."

Did she just say that or am I now hallucinating?
"After Doctor Gellhorn has performed your

procedure, Nurse Regina will issue you a jumbo Kotex and direct you to the recovery room. The recovery room is to the right. Nurse Apollo is in charge of the recovery room. She will assign you a cot on which to recover. Nurse Apollo is in love with Doctor Gellhorn. He accepts her invitations to dinner but never picks up the check and then demands unprotected sex from her. She means nothing to him."

Where is my video camera when I need it? This would go viral!

"There will be much moaning and crying in the recovery room but you should ignore anything you hear or see. If you moan or cry too much Nurse Apollo may have to ask you to leave. We do not want to upset anyone."

We don't want to upset anyone? What about me?

"Nurse Apollo will let you know when it's time to leave. You will proceed to the locker room and change back into your street clothes. Deposit the gown and slippers in the trash. Don't remove your jumbo Kotex. Your ride should meet you at the curb. Cell phones are not allowed in the clinic."

Ten

IT HURT LIKE HELL BUT IT WAS OVER FAST. I DON'T THINK Dr. Gellhorn made any dirty jokes—but then again I was only thinking of the pain. I don't remember much of anything until I heard Nurse Regina say to me, "It's time to get up; you will have time to grieve in the recovery room."

Then I found myself lying on a hard cot in the recovery room, weeping silently and thinking: this is my time to grieve. How much time will they give me? I thought about Aunt Sofia's funeral and the deafening silence of her family and the deadness in everyone's eyes. *So this is grief.*

None of the girls lying on the other cots made

eye contact, each desperately wanting this horror show to be over and to never speak of it again.

I still felt pregnant, all bloated and nauseous but now with terrible cramps as well. I felt like my entire insides were spilling out onto the jumbo Kotex.

Nurse Apollo came by every so often to change the Kotex and finally pronounced me fit to depart. I climbed back into my cutoffs and T-shirt and shuffled out to the lobby where Dad was reading a newspaper. He looked up. I think it was the first time he had looked at me since he had found out.

My father looked so much younger than any of my friends' fathers. Everyone always commented on how handsome he was—and how smart and successful. I felt proud when I heard people say that. I felt proud to have a father like him. That is why hurting my father was one of the worst things about getting pregnant. It made me sick to think about what I had done. I knew I had broken his heart.

"Ready to go?" he asked.

I nodded, silently, and followed him out to the car. As I walked out of that abortion clinic, I felt truly unforgivable, and that I was living an unforgivable life. I was a wretched, horrid person. Who could ever love or forgive someone like me? My life would forever remain in a state of undeniable pain, condemnation, and shame. I wanted to die.

Neither of us said a word all the way home. Dad concentrated on the road and I looked out the window, unable to focus on anything whizzing by.

//

When I got home I logged onto Facebook.

Aleecia: I got thrown out of the church choir. Apparently pregnant girls aren't fit to sing the Lord's praises.

Candy: Hypocritical bastards!

Aleecia: Now, I'm supposed to go for pastoral counseling with Father Rick.

Jasmine: Who is that?

Aleecia: He's a new junior minister. Just moved here from California. I heard that he is really hot.

Shawna: A hot minister? This could get interesting! Post photos.

Izzy: Check out this amazing video—In the womb.

Me: I can't look at that. I just had my abortion.

Shawna: How was it?

Me: Awful! The people working at the clinic were weird and creepy.

Shawna: I just found out that my mom had an abortion when she was seventeen. She said she thinks about the baby every day.

///

Dad told Mr. Rupczynski that I had a bad cold, and for the rest of the week, I spent a lot of time in the hammock, thinking. I lay there every day, staring at the fluffy clouds, thinking about Aunt Sofia walking into the river, wondering if my grandfather had raped Aunt Flo, and feeling sad for the baby that she had given up and the one that I had just killed.

I turned the camera on myself and started talking. "Abortion is a terrible thing, I have decided. It's not like just taking a dump and feeling better. You still have all those hormones and your breasts are sore and even though you knew you couldn't keep the baby, you still feel really sad and mournful. I only wish that people could see that abortion does not only hurt the little ones who get aborted but that it hurts us also in a very real, serious, and lasting way. I wish that people could see that with abortion in our lives we lose a kind of innate God-given blessedness, a life full of innocence and tenderness."

That video got four million views.

//

Nothing could erase the reality that I had been complicit in taking the life of my own baby. Rather than feeling relieved that the burden of my unborn child was eliminated, I felt twisted and changed. I felt haunted. *Too much death and loss for one summer*, I thought.

As requested, I had written up a list of the all boys I had sex with, in reverse chronological order starting with Chip, and gave it to Dad. My phone started to buzz with regularity as each boy received the summons to appear and provide a DNA sample. I imagined their parents' shock and anger as they dragged their sons one by one to the lab for the blood test—I knew their anger was directed toward me. The messages were just one-word texts: SLUT, CUNT, BITCH, WHORE. Nothing too original.

///

The next week I returned to my babysitting gig as though nothing had changed. But everything had changed.

"Rox," I said. "Let me see your profile."

"Will you help me with it?" she asked.

"Don't you think it's weird how dating profiles emphasize listings of your favorite TV shows, movies, and books?" I asked. "It's as if you are supposed to define yourself by how you distract yourself. It's like impersonating a person—this is what I do instead of being a person, instead of engaging with other people."

Roxanne just stared at me. She turned her monitor toward me so I could look at her profile.

Her handle was Roxy14 although she had listed her age as eighteen. OKCupid would have rejected her otherwise. Her profile included a couple of fetching selfies in her underwear, one topless. I guess it could have been worse.

I scanned through the thread of communications; all the guys were old, some in their fifties—older than my dad. *Gross! Who were these creeps trolling the Internet for underage girls?*

"Rox," I said. "You are a beautiful girl. And you

deserve to be loved. I don't think Isaac or any of these other guys loves you the way you deserve."

Roxanne's eyes got really big, "You're going to tell my dad, aren't you?"

"I'm trying to protect you," I said. "How do I do that? Help me."

"I want to have a boyfriend," she said.

"I understand that," I said. "The question is, how do we find a nice boy who is fourteen or maybe fifteen who thinks you're as great as I do?"

Okay, so I was laying it on thick. But, I didn't want her to end up like me.

"You don't need to have sex with a boy to make him love you," I said. I didn't really believe what I was saying. Did that unicorn exist—the guy who could love Roxanne unconditionally? Or me? Where was my unicorn? After what I had just been through, I wondered if I would be able to trust a man or let him get close to me, ever again.

I felt I needed to warn Roxanne. I needed her to learn how to trust herself enough to keep the men at bay until she was at least eighteen, and older if possible. I had read that women who stave off sexual relationships until they are nineteen or twenty tend to go further in their careers. They are better at choosing their partners and end up in stable, supportive relationships. Hell, even Mom fell for Dad when she was eighteen and regretted it the rest of her life.

"What if we take down your online profile and try to meet some boys at the pool?" I asked. "Or better yet, the tennis court. Let's find some doubles partners our own age. We'll put up a flyer: 'Teen girls seeking tennis partners.'"

"But I'm in love with Isaac," Roxanne protested. "And he loves me too."

"Do we know how old he is?" I asked. "Really?"

Eleven

THE NEXT DAY, I SHOWED UP FOR WORK AT EIGHT A.M. as usual and was surprised to see Mr. Rupczynski's car in the driveway. I wondered what was up.

I leaned my bike against the back wall of the house and opened the screen door to the kitchen.

Mr. Rupczynski and Roxanne were sitting at the table. Roxanne had her head buried in her arms and her shoulders were shaking with sobs.

"Who was that boy Mom saw you with at the mall?" Mr. Rupczynski asked.

Roxanne raised her head. Her face was streaked with tears and her eyes were swollen shut. "She's not my mom!" she bellowed. She folded her head back into her arms.

"Julia," Mr. Rupczynski said, frustrated. "Who did Julia see you with? She saw you get in his car and I need to know who he is. I promised Julia that you wouldn't cause any trouble this summer."

Just then Mr. Rupczynski noticed me standing awkwardly by the sink.

"Good morning, Luciana," he said. *Nobody calls me that anymore.* "Do you know about this boy that Roxanne has been seeing?"

"I don't know," I said. "What does he look like?"

"Julia said he was black," Mr. Rupczynski said. *Oh, geez. Isaac!*

Roxanne looked up at me, her eyes pleading.

I looked Mr. Rupczynski in the eye. "His name is Isaac. He works as a cook at a burger place downtown. *Big Bob's Burgers*, I think."

Roxanne screamed, "No!"

"I'm sorry, Roxanne," I said. "You know how

much I care about you. I am only looking out for you."

Mr. Rupczynski looked at me, sternly. "Why didn't you tell us about this?"

"Nothing happened that I'm aware of," I lied. "He showed up at the pool once and he left when I asked him to."

"You told him to leave?" Roxanne shrieked.

I shot Mr. Rupczynski an innocent look and he seemed to buy my story.

"Thank you, Luciana," Mr. Rupczynski said.

//

They arrested Isaac at work. He managed to text Roxanne before they took his phone away.

Isaac: The cops are here. What did you do?

Apparently he had outstanding warrants for unpaid child support and a petty theft charge—he had stolen five hundred dollars from his previous employer.

Roxanne texted me. Isaac got arrested.

I called the Linn County jail. They had a very helpful phone tree.

"For information on someone who has just been arrested, press four."

I pressed four. The robot voice said, "Transferring jail."

"County jail," a human voice said.

"I'm, um, trying to find out if my friend is there?" I said.

"Name?" the voice asked.

"Isaac Washington," I replied.

I heard her tapping on her computer keyboard. "Please hold," the voice said.

After a long time, she came back on the line. "He has been transferred to St. Luke's," the voice said.

"St. Luke's?" I asked. "What is St. Luke's?"

"St. Luke's Hospital," the voice said. The line went dead.

Isaac is at St. Luke's hospital, I texted Roxanne.

No!!! she replied.

I'll go down and see him, I texted back.

"Dad, I need to go visit someone in the hospital." At this point, I was under house arrest and Dad insisted on knowing where I was at all times.

"Who is in the hospital?" he shouted as the door slammed behind me.

I pedaled as fast as I could and locked my bike up outside the ER.

"I'm looking for Isaac Washington," I said to the clerk at the information booth.

She tapped a few strokes on her keyboard. "Room C-5," she said.

"Thanks!"

I wandered up and down the hall, confused by the room numbers. I almost walked by his room when I spotted him. He was on a ventilator and unconscious. An officer stood outside the door.

"You can't go in there," the cop said.

A nurse was walking out of his room. She was African-American.

I touched her arm.

"Excuse me?" I asked the nurse. "What happened?"

She gave a sideways glance at the police officer and said, "Not here."

I followed her to the nursing station.

"What happened to him?" I asked again.

"Rough ride," she said.

"What's that?" I asked.

"They toss these kids into the back of the police van but they don't strap them in. The driver careens all over town and slams on the breaks to make sure they go flying. We see these injuries all the time," she said. "Head trauma, spinal damage. It's just not right." She looked at me. "What's he in for?"

"Statutory rape," I said.

"White girl?" she asked.

"Yeah," I said. "Autistic."

"Oh, well that's just wrong," the nurse said.

"Yeah, but," I said. "Is he going to be okay?"

"Too soon to tell," she said.

On an impulse I walked back to Isaac's room where the door was still open. I whipped out my iPhone and started filming. It took a few minutes for the officer to notice but when he did, he lunged at me.

"Turn that off," he barked.

I turned the camera on him and caught him on video trying to grab my phone.

"Too late," I shouted as I ran down the corridor.

The video of Isaac's suffering in the hospital went viral on YouTube, which led to protests and an eventual inquiry into his death. Some officers were suspended but then life went on as usual.

///

"Hi, it's me. I think my babysitting career may be over. I feel really bad for Roxanne but I am glad Isaac is out of her life. May he rest in peace. I guess my role was to save her from predators like him. But I also knew she wouldn't be deterred, so in the end, I told her dad about her OKCupid profile. He packed Roxanne up and sent her back to her mother in Indianapolis."

"Roxanne's step-mom kind of freaked out. I hope I didn't cause some big problem for them. But, bottom line—theirs wasn't a marriage that was made to last. Mrs. Rupczynski was way out of her husband's league—her kids were so much cuter than his. And I'm also a little bit worried that this whole mess has had an impact on Dad's job. Geez, I sure hope not. But Dad just told me we are moving back to Pittsburgh at the end of the summer. So this is my last post from sunny Cedar Rapids."

Twelve

"**Y**OU ARE GOING TO HAVE TO TESTIFY," MOM SAID.

"I can't!" I cried. "I'm already a social pariah at school. Everybody is talking about me and all the boys who had to go for paternity tests!"

"Your father and I have been discussing that," Mom said. "You are not going back to Gateway High. We have transferred you to Central Catholic High."

"Catholic School?" I cried. "Mom, please!"

"Do you really want to go back to your school and face all those kids?" she snapped. "You have not only destroyed your reputation, you have humiliated your entire family."

Mom drove me to the deposition. The prosecuting attorney wore a cheap, poorly fitting pantsuit and too-high heels that were in need of repair. Her name was Ms. Delgado.

She led me into a bare conference room. The table was chipped and worn and the chairs were mismatched.

"Hello, Luciana. I am Ms. Delgado and I am going to be your attorney," she said.

That got us off to a bad start. I hate it when adults introduce themselves that way, like Ms. or Mr. She must have thought I couldn't read her business card, which said "Maria Delgado, Paralegal." Also, I knew what paralegal meant and it was not exactly attorney.

"Sit down Luciana," she said. "I am here to help you."

She gave me one of those sincere looks that I had never trusted.

"I want you to know that I don't judge you like the rest of the world might. I am here to be your advocate. You can tell me anything," she said.

I didn't want Ms. Delgado's scrutiny or advocacy. I stared at the nasty brown carpet and sulked. I thought about Maria, our cleaning lady. When our Maria got pissed at my mother, which happened pretty much every week, she would mutter under her breath, "Stick it where the sun don't shine." My mother always pretended not to hear, since she didn't want to have to clean the house herself. I had always loved that saying although I knew I would never have the nerve to actually say it. *Stick it where the sun don't shine, Ms. Delgado.*

"Will my mother be here?" I asked.

"No," Ms. Delgado said. "I'm afraid not."

"Good. I don't want her here. Will you tell her what I said?" I asked.

"No," she said. "Everything you tell me today will remain confidential. But, if the case goes to trial, she will probably be in the courtroom."

"I might have to go on trial?" I asked.

"You are not on trial—and, these cases usually settle," she said. "You have already established paternity of the aborted fetus and you are below the age of consent. Mr. Campbell doesn't have a case for pleading innocence."

Keith Campbell, my first. I remembered the back of the station wagon. "Will he go to jail?" I asked.

"Yes," she said. "In Pennsylvania, the penalty for having sex with someone under sixteen when you are four or more years older is up to ten years. You were fourteen, he was nineteen."

"Oh, God." I felt sick.

Ms. Delgado put her hand on my shoulder. "It's okay, sweetie. I just have a few questions. Are you ready to get started?"

I nodded.

"Tell me what happened on the night of May eighth," she said.

"Keith texted me and invited me to a party,"

I said. "He had just gotten back from school. He goes to college."

"Mr. Campbell?" she asked.

"Yes," I said. "Keith Campbell."

"Had you been acquainted with Mr. Campbell previously?" she asked.

"I met him at a party back in November when he was home for Thanksgiving," I said. "And I ran into him a few times over Christmas break at various parties."

At first I had loved the attention that Keith paid me. He was always surrounded by people, and I thought that by association, that made me popular. But when things got physical I realized that I didn't really like him at all. And thinking back, I realized the others probably didn't really like him, either. People hung around him because he always had drugs on him.

"At these parties," she asked. "Were you drinking alcohol?"

"Of course," I said. "We all were."

"And were you dancing topless?" she asked.

"Why?" I asked.

"You know, Luciana," Ms. Delgado said. "Sometimes you remind me of myself when I was your age."

I hate it when adults say stuff like that. It always came from someone you didn't want to be like. Frankly, I couldn't imagine Ms. Delgado dancing topless on a table at a house party.

I had to say something so I said, "Why is that?"

"I used to like to keep other people at arm's length too," she said. "I was afraid they wouldn't like me. So I stayed quiet and observed everyone from a distance. And when I said something, I made sure it was casual and funny and showed people that I didn't care about anything."

I didn't want to waste time listening to some kind of psychological mumbo-jumbo about myself, so I didn't say anything.

"Just tell me everything," she said. "The defense

may bring this up at trial and we want to be prepared."

I took a sip of water.

"So we have established that you went to a party with Mr. Campbell on the evening of May eighth. What happened next?"

"He drove to the party and parked out in front of the house," I said. "We were drinking vodka out of a water bottle. He started kissing me and putting his hands inside my bra. He kept telling me that he loved me and if I loved him too I would let him."

"Let him what?" Ms. Delgado asked.

"Let him have sex with me," I said.

"And did you?" she asked.

"We climbed into the way back of the station wagon," I said. "He had an air mattress and some blankets. He took off my clothes and we had sex."

It hurt, I remembered—him pushing and pushing. Me just lying there, waiting for it to be over. I heard his words in my head: "You're so beautiful."

"And then what happened?" she asked.

"We got dressed and went inside to the party," I said. "And afterward, he drove me home."

"Did you have sex with Mr. Campbell again?" she asked.

"Yes," I said. "Two more times."

"Have you had sex with other boys?" she asked.

"Yes," I said.

"Why did you do that?" Ms. Delgado asked.

"I wanted to be popular," I said. "I wanted them to like me."

"Isn't it true that seven boys received a summons to submit to a paternity test?" she asked.

If I had any guts I would have made up lots of big lies. Let her think all she wanted about me. She didn't know anything about me or my life.

"Yes," I said.

She gave me one of those big, sympathetic smiles and I felt like I was drowning in molasses.

"I just want to clarify," she said. "None of this matters. There is no such thing as consensual sex with a minor. You were fourteen and not old enough to give consent. The defense may bring up these kinds of questions to upset you and rattle you. They will try to portray you as promiscuous. I want you to be prepared for this line of questioning."

"I really don't want to testify," I said. I began to cry again. "A lot of kids from school will be there watching."

Thirteen

"**L**UCI, DID YOU REALLY WANT TO CLIMB INTO THE BACK of the station wagon?" Ms. Delgado asked.

"No," I replied. "Not, really."

"Did you enjoy the sex?" she asked.

"No," I said. "I hated it. I hated myself."

Ms. Delgado put her arm around me. "Are you getting help?" she asked.

"What kind of help?" I asked.

"Therapy?" she said. "Counseling?"

"I have a YouTube channel," I said. "You should check it out—I have five million followers now."

"A YouTube channel?" she asked. "How is that like therapy?"

"I talk and people listen and comment," I said. "It's called *Luci9Months*. I got the idea from a Facebook page I found a couple of months ago. All these pregnant teens are on there sharing their stories and supporting each other. Now we have *Nine Months*—the YouTube version. I interview teens and we talk about everything: boys' hormones and anatomy, that sort of thing—orgasms, birth control, pregnancy, abortion, adoption, birth, marriage, and raising a baby. It's amazing. You should check it out!"

She gave me a startled look and glanced down at her notebook.

"I'm serious," I said. "I still think about my aborted baby every day and don't want anyone else to have to go through such a horror-show. I am a cautionary tale, right? I am on a mission to teach teens about the realities and consequences of being sexual."

"I think that's all for today," she said. "I'll let your mother know if we need you in court, but like I said, these cases usually settle."

//

Ms. Delgado was right; Keith settled the case and received a sentence of ten years. The next thing I heard he had overdosed and died. *R.I.P. motherfucker.*

//

Catholic school was a joke. Plaid, pleated skirt, white polo shirt, and knee socks. *Seriously? Knee socks?* I felt like a Japanese businessman's idea of a kiddie-porn fantasy girl.

My YouTube followers were tweeting my videos and a lot of the freshman class at Central Cath was already following me. Every day, I would get texts from girls offering to be interviewed on camera about their predicament. Because as it turned out there were a lot of pregnant girls in Catholic School.

I set up a studio stage in my bedroom with two white wicker chairs and a side table that I had purchased at Pier1. The format was basically Ellen DeGeneres meets Zach Galifianakis's *Between Two Ferns* except that I wasn't a lesbian and I didn't have any ferns in my bedroom. I set up a tripod in the corner of my bedroom with my new camera, a high-level Canon 60D with a flattering lens, a step up from the built-in webcam on my Mac that I used for my videos in Iowa. Sometimes I used professional lights to record, but mostly I shot in the natural light that came in through my bedroom window. I also owned a high-quality microphone but it didn't get used much either. I would shoot videos on the street and on the subway and standing in hotel elevators. Really, you know, a video can happen anywhere.

///

On a typically warm, sunny afternoon after school, I sat down in my bedroom "studio," pressed record, then waved my arms around.

"Now we are in a Luci video!" I said. It had become my hallmark delivery—a lilting, cheerleader kind of voice. "Yay, videos!"`

"Hello everyone," I said into the camera. "Today I would like to introduce Dana."

Dana had short, straight brown hair and dark eyes. She was the kind of girl people referred to as perky. She couldn't wait to get in front of the camera and start talking about how much she still loved her boyfriend.

"Some of you have heard this all before," she started. She sounded kind of apologetic but she didn't stop talking. "But Jimmy and I have been together forever. I mean, we have been going together since the seventh grade, and we have always loved each other. I have thought about it a lot, and I really don't think the baby could make him stop loving me."

Dana held a tissue in her hands and she kept twisting it around while she talked. The longer she talked the more she twisted it. "Jimmy still loves me," she said. "I know he still loves me. And he is going to love our baby, too. It's just taking him time to realize that. I know it must seem strange to everybody that we are apart right now. But it's just a temporary thing. We are going to be back together soon."

I felt sick all of a sudden and paused the camera. *Dana, why don't you just rip your heart out right here in front of everyone as long as you are at it?* Was she going to have a nervous breakdown? My mother had two nervous breakdowns and I did not like being around her while that was going on.

Dana looked at me. "Is it on?" I nodded and resumed shooting.

"I haven't heard from Jimmy in several weeks.

But that does not mean that he doesn't love me. It just means that he is going through a hard time right now." Dana bowed her head and stared at her tissue. "Though, I did hear he was dating someone else." Her voice dropped to a whisper. "Someone told me that."

Dana looked back up at the camera and spoke louder. "But I don't believe it. I know he still loves me and we will get married and we will keep our baby."

Dana stifled a sob. "I can hope, can't I? It's better to hope, isn't it?"

She looked directly at me but I didn't know what to say so she answered her own question. "Yes, it's much better to hope. I know that. It's always better to hope."

I kept the camera trained on her face as she started to cry and kept trying to smile at the same time. I zoomed in as a tear slid down her cheek and onto her dress.

Yeah, Dana's parents, you are so lucky! You have

a daughter that documents her whole life and puts it up on YouTube for you guys to view!

That video got seven million views.

//

The doorbell rang.

"Thanks, Dana," I said. "That was awesome! But I think my next guest is here."

I walked Dana to the door.

"I hope Jimmy comes back," I whispered as I hugged her goodbye. "I really do."

In the doorway stood Eve, a tall, thin girl with her hair in a long ponytail and beautiful sad eyes.

"You must be Eve?" I asked.

She smiled, exposing a gap between her two front teeth.

"Welcome to my studio!" I said.

She followed me upstairs to my room.

"I will probably post this segment tomorrow, if it's okay with you?" I said as I fiddled with the camera. "I just posted Dana's segment and we want your segment to get all the exposure it deserves, right?"

I looked at Eve. She nodded eagerly.

Fourteen

"**A**LRIGHTY THEN!" I SAID INTO THE CAMERA. "NOW we are in a Luci video! I would like to introduce Eve!"

I turned the camera on Eve. She waved frantically.

"Eve, tell us how you found out," I said.

"This is so embarrassing!" Eve giggled and pressed her hand to her mouth. "I was at the beach with my friend Liz complaining as usual about being flat-chested."

I trained the camera on Eve's boobs for a few seconds and then back on her face.

"And my friend Liz told me about the pill.

She said that if I went on the pill it could move me up a full cup size! And she said I could go to Planned Parenthood and get a prescription for the pill without even telling my parents. So of course I did that. I was having sex with Tony anyway, so it seemed like a good idea. After school I drove over, singing out the window of my car like a freaking idiot while visions of C-cups bounced in my head. When I got there, they made me take a blood test and it said I was already pregnant. The thought had not even occurred to me. That's how much of a dumbass I was."

I turned the camera back on me.

"See girls, it can happen to the best of us!" I said cheerfully. "Eve has a three-point-nine GPA—imagine that!"

I turned the camera back on Eve.

"Eve, does Tony know?" I asked.

"He is kind of a dumbass, too," she said.

"Are you going to tell him?" I asked.

"I've . . . I need to figure everything out," she said.

"You don't want to tell him?" I asked. "Is Tony your boyfriend?"

"No!" she said. "He is just some guy from school that I use for sex."

I kept the camera trained on Eve for five seconds. She grinned her gap-tooth smile.

Eve's video got four million views.

"Who is watching this?" Eve asked.

"My audience is made up of girls generally between eleven and seventeen," I said.

"Eleven," she repeated. "That seems kind of young!"

"At first that surprised me too," I said. "I thought I was making videos for my peers—girls our age. In my mind, my videos sometimes are inappropriate for an eleven-year-old. But that's what they're watching."

///

Despite my anything-goes brashness on camera, I cared very much about my responsibility as a role model. After Eve had left, I scrolled through the comments on my videos, and regularly found notes from girls as young as nine. *I sure hope my youngest fans are at least watching with an adult,* I thought. *But apparently most aren't.* When one parent commented on a recent video that the language was inappropriate for young girls and asked that it be taken down, my comment thread was swarmed by teenagers, defending me.

Seriously, I'm thirteen. You need to understand that we watch Luci, we swear, we think wrong, we act insane, we have Facebooks, we can't live without Internet, we can't live without our phones. THAT'S JUST THE WAY IT IS!! I never watch television. I would rather watch Luci's show all day than anything else. She swears a lot, but she's funny.

That inspired me to keep going. Next up: Holly.

Holly had brown hair and freckles. She talked in a coal-country drawl, so bad it made Roxanne sound like the Queen of England. Her eyes were already red when she arrived, like she had just finished crying.

"Yay videos!" I said and then turned the camera on Holly.

"Should I start?" Holly asked.

"Yep," I said. "You are on camera. Tell us your story."

"Well," Holly said, drawn out and slow, like the word had three syllables. "I always knew that it was the best thing to give up my baby. I didn't have any real doubts. My family is real poor."

How did she get into Catholic School in Pittsburgh, I wondered?

"My momma sent me here to stay with her sister."

Holly seemed to be reading my mind.

"She works at the school. In the kitchen," she added. "Anywho."

I have always hated that word—anywho!

"There's no way we could afford another mouth to feed," Holly said. "Those were my mama's words. Besides, my daddy's got problems. He beat me up bad when he found out. I could just imagine what he would do to my poor child. He beat me with a razor strap—for my own good, he says. He drinks too much and he has a terrible temper. I am scared to death of him."

I thought about what my dad had told me about his father: *When he was drunk and in one of his rages, he would drag one of the older girls upstairs and do only God knows what.*

"But, now I am thinking more and more about the baby. I can feel it moving inside of me. I can't bear the thought of giving it up and never knowing where it lives and what it's doing. How can I do that?"

Then the waterworks burst forth and I handed her a tissue.

"Thank you," Holly says. She looked into the camera again. "How can I give my baby up? How can I?"

Somewhere inside me, I could feel a part of me aching. I didn't want to feel this. I don't want to feel anything. I want to tell her that it's better not to think about the baby. She shouldn't be thinking about keeping it, either.

She looked directly into the camera. "My boyfriend wanted to marry me. He did."

I find this hard to believe.

"But I knew it would be a mistake. I didn't want to end up like my mama. She's not even forty but she looks so old and tired and worn out from having too many children."

She stared off into space so I paused the camera. "Are you done?" I asked.

"How was that?" Holly asked. Suddenly she

was completely dry-eyed. Was this all an act? What an actress!

"Good—real good," I said. "Are you going to be okay?" I asked.

"When will it be posted?" she asked.

"Today," I said. "I'll send you the link so you can see how many views it gets."

"Thank you," she said. There was no trace of hillbilly in her voice. Who is this girl, I thought? Is this an audition video that we had just made?

The video got two hundred thousand views and thirty comments.

One of the comments came from Holly: "My baby died. The doctors don't know why. Just one of those things, they said. She lived for three hours. They said she didn't suffer. Maybe it was for the best."

After Holly posted her comment, the views jumped to two million.

I can't figure it out. I don't know why I feel so terrible. I don't even know Holly and I think she was probably playing me. Nobody wanted that baby. It was a mistake from the beginning. What difference does it make that it had died?

Fifteen

MY REPUTATION HAD SPREAD WAY BEYOND MY HIGH school and women from all over the greater Pittsburgh area were contacting me via my Facebook page. I chose Carol as my next victim.

"Yay videos!"

"Hi, I'm Carol." Carol looked like a blonder version of me, with a big white grin. She had great teeth. I could tell she knew it, too. She was also an extrovert. If there was anything I hated, it was an extrovert. To hear her talk, she was the most popular coed in the history of the University of Pittsburgh.

"Some nights I even had two dates," she said.

"My sorority sisters were so jealous, they wanted to kill me."

What stopped them? I wondered.

"I've always been well-dressed," Carol said into my camera. "Grooming is important to me. And what is it with maternity clothes—can you believe how poorly made they are? I can't find a thing to wear! There's nothing out there that is remotely flattering." Carol laughed like she was saying something hilarious. I rolled my eyes but she didn't seem to notice.

Okay. I know what you are thinking—I never made it far enough to need maternity clothes. Who am I to judge? Maybe Carol had a point. But by then she had launched into a discussion of beauty tips.

"What's the secret to beauty when you are pregnant?" she asked the camera. "Vaseline. The most important thing you can do is to rub Vaseline on your belly. That will help get rid of the stretch marks. In a few months, you're going to be back out there on the dating scene and you will need to pretend that none of this ever happened. How are you going to pretend to your next boyfriend that you never had a baby?"

And then Carol said something that threw me for a loop.

"You would have to be a fool to trust a man. You might as well throw your life away. Men want sex; that is all. Once they get it, they leave you and they do not give a damn about what happens to you. They will break your heart if you let them."

Carol looked angry. She was practically glaring at the camera.

"We need to get what we can out of men—the same way they get what they can out of us. I want a life that is better than my mother's and you tell me how I am going to do that without a man. You can control men—or you can let them control you."

I switched off the camera. "Thank you, Carol,"

I said. "I'll send you the link to the video once I've posted it."

"But I am not done!" Carol protested.

"I'm sorry," I lied. "That's all we have time for today." I escorted Carol downstairs to the door.

I felt like I needed to take a walk, or just find a quiet place to think my thoughts. *Where is my hammock when I need it?* I sat on the back porch and smoked a cigarette. I was not sure if I would post the video. Carol's comments didn't seem to fit into my meme. *What is my meme?* And then it dawned on me: I would splice the audio files from several of my videos together and set it to a rap beat.

//

You would have to be a fool to trust a man.
Jimmy still loves me.
I can feel it moving inside of me.
There's no way we could afford

another mouth to feed.
He is just some guy from school
that I use for sex.
You might as well throw your life away.
How can I give my baby up? How can I?
I know he still loves me.
You can control men—
or you can let them control you.
I can hope, can't I?
It's better to hope, isn't it?

//

"We're in a Luci video, I would like to introduce Peggy. Peggy, tell us about your abortion."

"My abortion happened last year when I was sixteen. I was dating Joey, a guy that I loved very much but just before my abortion, we had a fight and broke up—for good. I had found out that he was dealing drugs and I wanted him out of my life. Wouldn't you know it, two weeks later,

I found out that I was pregnant. When I told Joey, he said that he wanted me to have an abortion because he didn't think I would be a good mother. He paid for my abortion with his drug money." Peggy looked down at her hands, which were folded in her lap.

"Peggy, do you need a minute?" I asked.

She shook her head and looked up. "The night before my abortion, I couldn't sleep. I was lying alone in bed with my own thoughts, and I knew what I was about to do was very wrong. In the morning I went to the abortion clinic by myself. There were picketers in front so I drove around the block wanting to make sure that I didn't recognize anyone. None of them looked familiar, so I pulled into the parking lot and went in. The picketers yelled stuff to me, but I felt they didn't know my situation so they didn't deserve my time."

"Of course not," I said, off-camera.

"I gave the receptionist a fake name. I felt

numb. I filled out paperwork, talked to a counselor, talked to a nurse, and tried not to think about what I was doing. A nurse escorted me into the abortion room. She helped me get ready for the procedure and just asked me vague questions about the weather and if I was going to school. Then the abortionist came into the room and began my abortion. The nurse was leaning over me and staring into my eyes. After a little while, she asked the doctor 'Is something wrong?' I heard him say, 'It's trying to get away—I've tried three times!'"

I couldn't help it, I gasped. *Does that really happen?*

"I was shocked!" Peggy said.

"Well, yeah!" I exclaimed.

"It is trying to get away!" he repeated. "I started to pray and ask God to stop all this from happening—to not let it work—to let it fail—to put His hand in the way of the doctor's vacuum. I couldn't believe what I was doing! And then the abortionist said, 'It's done.' He put away his tools and left the room. From that moment on I have regretted my abortion! I just wanted to run, to die . . . I was so angry! After the nurse left the room, I started to cry. A part of me died in that room. I knew what I did was wrong. The *it* he was referring to was *my baby*!"

I leaned over and gave Peggy a hug on-camera.

"As I walked out of there, I just bawled. I remember looking at the sky, wondering what God thought of me. The rest of the day, I laid on the couch. I wanted to go back to that place and pull my baby out of the dumpster. If only I could live that day over again. My decision to have an abortion was final. It was over. I can't go back.

"I named my baby Baby Christy and I wrote her a letter. I still have things that make me grieve, like when I go to the dentist and hear the suction machine. My abortion happened two days before Valentine's Day, so every Valentine's Day is a reminder. Baby Christy would have been born in September. By now, she would be two years old. I wonder what she would look like. I wonder what her laugh would sound like. I will never be able to hold her or kiss her goodnight. To tell her I am sorry. I can't believe that I took the life of an innocent baby to make myself look better. I really wish I had had the courage to stand up for Baby Christy and said *no*."

Peggy continued in a soft voice. "My grief drew me closer to God. I know that He forgives me for what I did. When I asked for His forgiveness, He gave me a clean slate. He remembers my sin no more. For that, I am eternally grateful! I know that, when I die, God will welcome me in to Heaven. Standing next to Him will be Baby Christy. Only then will I no longer regret my abortion."

Peggy sobbed silently as the camera continued to record.

"Thank you, Peggy," I said at last. "Thank you for sharing your story."

Sixteen

POSTED PEGGY'S VIDEO AFTER SUPPER THAT EVENING AND by the next morning it had received three million views and over five hundred comments. *Wow! I am onto something here!* I sifted through my emails and looked for another girl who wanted to share her abortion story. I found one—Heather!

//

"Heather, you're in a Luci video," I said. "Tell us about your abortion. How old were you?"

Heather looked at me and said, "I was fourteen."

"Look into the camera, Heather," I said.

She looked into the camera and repeated, "I was fourteen."

"Tell us your story," I coaxed.

"I wasn't forced into an abortion. My boyfriend did not threaten to leave me. Actually, he made me promise I wouldn't do it. I had actually tried to get pregnant—which seems crazy at fourteen, but I have been struggling with depression for what seems like forever, and I wanted to feel needed. And for two months I was—I was needed. Never in my life was I as happy as when I took the pregnancy test. I cried tears of joy and jumped around. It was magical!" Heather beamed at the memory.

Then her smile faded. "My mother had already made the decision for me. I cried for days before the appointment, and I cried the entire way there. I knew this was not what I wanted, but it was all happening so fast. It was truly traumatizing. It has been two years, and I still can't go into a doctor's office without thinking about it."

Heather gazed out the window and said, "You

rarely hear mothers say that they regret having their little bundle of joy, but you hear all of the time that people regret their abortions."

"All the time," I agreed.

Heather looked into the camera and said forcefully, "I am not one hundred percent against abortion, which will probably get this video taken down, but I have never made a bigger mistake in my entire life and probably never will. This will stay with me even when I grow up and have another child."

"I just wish I could go back and tell myself to quit being selfish. But it's too late. I have already made my mistake."

Selfish—I had never thought about it that way. Had I been selfish?

"What about your boyfriend?" I asked. "Is he still in the picture?"

"He was pissed that I broke my promise," Heather said. "He said he could never forgive me. I think that is part of the reason I feel so bad."

"Thank you, Heather," I said and switched off the camera. "Do you need a hug?"

"That's okay," she said, suddenly calm. "When will you post it?"

"Today," I said. "I'll send you a link that you can share with your mom if you like."

Heather looked at me, quizzically. "My mom?"

"Did you ever tell your mom all this?" I asked. "How you feel?"

"No," Heather said. "She wouldn't understand."

"Tell her to check out my YouTube channel," I said. "There are lots of stories like yours."

"I'll think about it," Heather said as she stood to leave.

That video got four million views and Heather's mother posted a comment: "You are my brave girl. I love you. Mom."

//

"We're in a Luci video, I'd like to introduce Crystal."

Crystal waved at the camera.

"Crystal, tell us about your abortion."

"I found out I was pregnant when I was in high school—my junior year. I was only seventeen, and my boyfriend and I had only been together for two or three months at that time. I remember finding out in the morning, before school. I was getting morning sickness and throwing up and gaining weight. I knew something was wrong, but I ignored it. My sister bought me a test, and I took it in the morning before school. It came out positive, and I broke down crying—trying to figure out what I was going to do and how I was going to tell my family and my boyfriend."

"I told my boyfriend after school when he picked me up. He broke down crying. My mom was next, and she was so mad at me. She just kept saying, 'What are you going to do now?' Two days went by and my boyfriend and I started talking about options. We both decided on an abortion."

"I got my abortion when I was three months pregnant—on my boyfriend's birthday. That way we'll always remember the date. As soon as they put the needle in my arm, I knew I didn't want to do it, but I was just so scared and then I blacked out from the medicine. I woke up feeling really dizzy and in pain."

"And how do you feel, now?" I asked.

"It was the biggest mistake of my life. If I could, I would go back and undo it. To this day, I still don't forgive myself. I know my baby was going to be a little girl. We gave her a name. Her name is Caitlyn. Every year on my boyfriend's birthday we will light a candle for Caitlyn."

Crystal looked into the camera, "Caitlyn, Mommy and Daddy love you. I'm sorry, my love. I wish I could hold you in my arms right now, but I know God is taking good care of you."

I started to tear up and zoomed the camera in

on my face to catch my expression. Why hadn't I named my baby? I'm sure I could go back and find the date in my calendar. I could have a little ceremony for my baby every year. I found that idea strangely comforting.

"So you and you boyfriend are still together?" I asked.

"We're planning to get married and some day we want to have a family," Crystal said.

"Thank you Crystal," I said and switched off the camera.

That video got three million views.

//

"Yay videos! My guest today is Georgiana. Tell us your story."

"Hi, I'm Georgiana," she said. "I was on the pill and my period was late. I was spotting, but I thought it would eventually come. Then I started to feel sick—nauseated and all—and I realized something was wrong. One day I decided to take a test, and my worst fear confronted me. I was sixteen and pregnant. I told myself I would have an abortion. I really did not think there was any other option."

"I told my boyfriend and he agreed to take me to the clinic. But they were having a power outage—we were having rolling blackouts at the time. So we went back home. I wondered if it was a sign—maybe I wasn't supposed to get an abortion? But the following day we went back again."

"We didn't know how far along I was. When they did the sonogram—it was so cute and so tiny. I fell in love with it right there and then. We were told I was six weeks and five days. The due date would have been in February. Aquarius—that's my favorite sign! They gave me a print of the sonogram; I just wanted to cry. I was hurting so much that I wanted to stop the process, but I knew I could not keep the baby. I was only sixteen."

"We had to go to another clinic where they

had to put the pill inside of me. The second doctor was rude when he told me to take off my clothes—telling me to hurry up. He never gave me any counseling or anything. I was not happy about how I was treated. I felt like I was being judged, but nobody asked why I was doing this or if we had thought about other options."

"I went home hurting. The bleeding started; the pain started; I cried. The blood clots came out and I felt like I was dying. I had to go back the following day for cleaning. All I could think about was my baby."

"We were told there was only one doctor—I sat in the waiting room for hours in pain. The girl in front of me looked very young—maybe twelve? When she was in the procedure room I could hear screaming and I got really scared. The doctor—this time a different one—was a little bit nicer. He said I would be fine as he injected me with anesthetic. I do not remember anything after that. I woke up in the recovery room. It had been done, I was in pain, and I was still dizzy.

"Now the horror of everything is coming back to me. I miss my baby, though I thought I had no other option. It is breaking my heart. Every time I am alone, I cry. Every time I see a baby, I think about my baby. What if I cannot have another child? I will never forgive myself."

Georgiana looked directly into the camera and took on a stern tone. "Anyone thinking of aborting—think twice before you do it. I cannot change it; my baby is gone, and there is a big hole in my heart that is reminding me no one can make me feel the same way as I did when I saw my baby on the sonogram."

"Do you have any other advice for our viewers?" I asked.

"I really think places like Planned Parenthood need to provide patients with more information—specifically about the aftermath of what may happen to one's emotional state. All they inform you of is what happens during the procedure and that is it. I do not think places like this should exist at all. I am now one hundred percent anti-abortion."

"Thank you Georgiana," I said. "I know that was hard for you."

"I want to do what I can to help others in this situation in any way I can," she said. "I want my voice to be heard. I am no longer ashamed of what I did, but will always regret what I did. Regret dies hard."

Georgiana's voice was heard by three million people.

Seventeen

"WE'RE IN A LUCI VIDEO. MY GUEST TODAY IS FAITH. Hi, Faith, tell us about your abortion."

"Hi!" Faith waved at the camera. "I had my abortion when I was fourteen weeks along."

"How old are you?" I asked.

"Seventeen," she answered. "And I was so unsure about my decision for the entire three months I was pregnant. But, I felt so much pressure from my family members and my boyfriend, and I unfortunately gave in. I made the decision to have an abortion based on the fact that my boyfriend meant the world to me, and I knew I would lose him if I chose to keep the baby. I have cried each and every day since, and I wish I could go back to that day and tell them that I didn't want to do it."

"And where is your boyfriend, now?" I asked.

"I broke up with my boyfriend and haven't had anything to do with him since," Faith said.

"Before the procedure, I saw an ultrasound of my baby. My little girl or boy was on the screen, and I could see their little head and body. That is an image I will never forget. I will live with regret every single day of my life, and I would give anything to have my baby back. I wish I had listened to my heart and chosen to continue my pregnancy. I wish I were able to see my child grow, and hold my child, and see their little face. I have never experienced heartache like this before, and I know I will never forget it. If anyone watching is in a similar situation, I really hope that you follow your heart and make the right decision for you. The most painful thing is seeing all of the people who pressured you being completely unaffected, while you are dying inside. Men will leave and treat you badly, and I truly regret allowing a man to convince me to kill my baby, because no other person is worth losing my child over."

"How are you coping with the loss?" I asked.

"I learned that it helps for me to think about the time I spent with her. It was not a long time and I never felt her move, but my body knew she was there. I was sick for all three months—not just morning sickness but all day! It was terrible and wonderful at the same time. I craved Buffalo chicken wings every night at midnight. I would wake up and want them so bad and giggle because that was what she wanted. I also craved orange juice and grape Kool-Aid for all three months. I could not stand to eat chocolate or onions—the smell made me want to throw up. I would wake up every morning holding my stomach and smiling. I would give anything to feel it all again."

"I am sure you will get another chance," I said. "Thank you, Faith, for sharing your story."

My YouTube following was now nearing five million.

//

Amanda was a girl in my religion class who never spoke up or even raised her hand. Whenever the nun called on her she turned beet-red, all the way up to her reddish hairline, and I realized that she was horribly shy. That is why I was surprised when she approached me one day in the hallway.

"Luci?" she said. "My name is Amanda. I am in your religion class?"

"I know, Amanda," I said.

"You do?" Amanda said. "Wow! I didn't know anybody knew my name."

"Did you want something?" I asked.

"I want to make a video," Amanda said.

"Are you pregnant?" I asked. Let's face it, I was shocked. Amanda did not seem like the kind of girl that would get much attention from boys. Even Catholic School boys.

She nodded, eagerly. We ran back to my house as soon as the final bell rang.

"Now we're in a Luci video! I would like to introduce Amanda!"

"We never talked about sex at my house," Amanda said into the camera. Her face was bright red. "I am the oldest kid in my family, so I didn't have any older brothers or sisters to tell me anything. I was eleven when I got my period. I thought I was sick, and told my mother I needed to go to the hospital. That must sound funny to you but I didn't know what was wrong with me. I thought maybe I was dying. My mother gave me a Kotex and talked to me about keeping clean. But she didn't tell me anything about sex and having babies. I didn't find out about it until I was fourteen and I got pregnant. I thought you had to be married to have babies. That's how stupid I was. I thought you had to love each other."

"You're not stupid," I said, off-camera. "It wasn't your fault that your parents didn't tell you the facts of life. How could you have known?" I thought about how my mother talked to me about sex the year my period started. I was eleven at the time, just like Amanda. My mother told me I was a woman now and that was wonderful. After that she told me about all kinds of strange things like penises and vaginas, and she used the word *intercourse*. The way I imagined it, the man came and stuck his penis in you and then he walked off. That didn't sound so great to me. It sounded a lot like getting a shot at the doctor's office. I knew it wasn't going to be a problem for me to avoid intercourse until I got married. After that, I just hoped you didn't have to do it too often.

"Father William is the father," Amanda said.

I had been lost in my thoughts but I bolted to attention. "A priest?" I asked off-camera. "Did you say that your baby's father is a priest?"

"Pastor," Amanda said. "I am Episcopalian."

That just takes the cake, as my mother would say. I imagined Father William jumping Amanda while quoting some verse from the Bible about how you're supposed to spread your legs to receive Holy Communion by special delivery. Poor Amanda!

"You must think I am a terrible person for sleeping with my pastor," Amanda said into the camera. "Religion has always been important to me. Church always made me feel happy and peaceful. Father William is our new minister. He's in his thirties and everyone loves him. His wife is young too, and their two kids are adorable. When they came here, they put so much energy into the church. I helped with Sunday school and the children's choir. I just felt happy every time I was there. I felt like everyone there liked me, especially Father William. I went to the church a lot on Saturdays. Usually there were other people there. We would all help clean the church or put up special decorations. But one Saturday, I went there and everyone else had already left. Father William and

I were the only ones there. We worked together and cleaned up the sanctuary. After a while Father William said we should stop and rest. So we sat down on the floor. Both of us were dusty and dirty. I was sitting there laughing and talking with him and I kept thinking that I wished my dad was more like Father William. Then I started wishing that Father William was my dad. I could tell he liked me and I can't imagine what it would be like to have a dad who liked you."

I kept the camera trained on Amanda, trying really hard to keep my hand from shaking.

"He told me that I had dirt in my hair and took out his handkerchief to wipe it off. Then he dropped the handkerchief and all of a sudden he was stroking my hair—very softly. He told me that he loved me. He said he couldn't stop himself because he loved me. He started taking off my clothes and I didn't know what to do. He loved me! That was what he said! I know I should have stopped him. I kept saying no and he would say, 'Shhhh,' and put his finger on my lips. He said it was all good and right because we loved each other. I knew it wasn't right but I couldn't stop it. And then when it was over he acted different. He seemed like a different person. He told me I had to hurry up and get dressed. He looked at me like I was some kind of slut. He had never looked at me like that before. I kept waiting for him to say something. But he didn't. He just wanted me to leave."

"Did you tell your mother?" I asked.

"She didn't believe me," Amanda said. "She said I was accusing this fine man, and that I was a liar and a whore. I had never heard that word before."

"What are you going to do?" I asked.

"My family doesn't believe in abortion. They sent me here to Catholic School until the baby is born," Amanda said. "The nuns will take the baby away and give it to a family."

I turned off the camera and regarded Amanda solemnly. This project had taken an unexpected turn.

"Will you post my video?" Amanda asked expectantly.

"Do you want me to?" I asked.

"Oh, yes!" she said.

"But it might get the pastor in trouble," I said. "Is that what you want?"

I thought of the seven boys who had been subpoenaed for paternity tests. I thought about Keith Campbell and felt remorse. Death by overdose whether accidental or deliberate was a punishment that certainly did not fit the crime. What would happen to Father William? I suddenly became aware of the power I wielded via YouTube. I was like the Perez Hilton for teen preggos. I could alter people's lives forever. On the other hand, why should Amanda be condemned for the actions of a full-grown—not to mention married—man? What was my liability here? What if Amanda was lying?

"I'm not lying, you know," Amanda said.

Okay. She's a mind reader, too. "Yes, I'll post the video this week," I said. "I'll send you the link when it's live but you might not want to read the comments. They can be very harsh."

I posted the video with grave misgivings. It got ten million views. Father William was searched four million times on Google.

Eighteen

THE CONVERSATION WITH AMANDA GOT ME THINKING: DID I want my vlog to become the America's Most Wanted of statutory rapists? Or was my mission to give voice to teens who chose to keep their babies? And then a light bulb went off. What if I did a whole series around my Facebook friends: Jasmine, Candy, Shawna, Izzy and Aleecia? They all were kids raising babies on their own. I wonder how that was working out for them?

I logged onto Facebook.

Me: Have you guys been following my YouTube channel?

Jasmine: You're on YouTube?

Me: Check it out—Luci9Months. I was thinking of building a series around you ladies. What do you think? We could call it Real Teen Moms.

Aleecia: Like Real Housewives?

Me: Exactly!

//

"Welcome to *Real Teen Moms* brought to you by Luci Video," I said into the camera. "Yay, videos!"

I had changed out the format a bit. My remote guests were beamed in via webcam, which I controlled via remote and monitored on my iPad. I set up the video feed as a split screen on my monitor so that it looked like we were in the same room.

"Our first guest is Jasmine Walker." I looked down at my notes. "Jasmine was nineteen and a student at the University of Nevada at Las Vegas when she found out she was pregnant. She has a beautiful daughter named Orchid, who is now eighteen months old. Jasmine will share her amazing journey of how she lost and fought to regain custody of her child. Welcome Jasmine!"

I imagined thunderous applause emanating from the studio audience accompanied by the thumping beat of a pop song. I zoomed the camera out to frame Jasmine and Orchid, who was sitting in her lap. They were dressed in matching mother-daughter outfits in dusty blue silk.

"Well, don't you two look beautiful!" I said.

"Thanks," Jasmine said. "This is the dress I was wearing the night I conceived Orchid. I know it may seem crazy but it's still my favorite dress. And I bought some of the same material to make a little dress for Orchid. I think it brings out the blue in her eyes."

"You both look amazing!" I imagined myself as a young Amy Schumer. Then I channeled Ellen: "Jasmine, tell us about your journey."

"Thanks Luci," Jasmine said. "Like you said, I was an undergraduate at UNLV and working as a showgirl in a review when I was date-raped at a cast party."

"Do you want to tell us about the birth father?" I asked.

"My lawyer tells me that I can't talk about him," she said. "We have settled that matter and he is the reason I was able to get my daughter back." Jasmine rested her head affectionately on Orchid's, who was staring into the void with wide eyes.

"I hope my story can inspire other teen moms to fight the system and do what is right for their babies," Jasmine said. "So, yeah, I got pregnant, unexpectedly, but when I found out, I decided to have the baby." She smiled and bounced Orchid in her lap.

"So you never considered abortion as an option?" I asked.

"I wasn't raised that way," Jasmine said. "It's not like my mom is a big church-goer, but she is strongly pro-life. When I was in high school, she used to drag me to marches in front of the Planned Parenthood office in Hackensack."

"So you decided on adoption?" I asked.

"Not at first," Jasmine said. "I was planning to find a job and finish school. But it was hard, really hard trying to raise my baby alone. I was struggling to keep up with school and pay the rent and I didn't have anyone to watch Orchid while I was out looking for work." Jasmine took a pause. "I think that's one thing that a lot of young girls don't take into account. Child care is expensive— so you either need to have money or family around to take care of your baby."

"So what did you do?" I asked.

"I made a really tough decision—I gave my baby up for adoption." Jasmine paused for dramatic effect.

Damn! Why didn't we have a studio audience to record their response?

"I left Orchid in Las Vegas with a really nice family and moved back to New Jersey to try to get on with my life. But I thought about Orchid every day," Jasmine said. "When they tell you that you should give your baby up for adoption, they also tell you that you are doing the right thing for your child and that knowledge will help you get over it. But it's not like giving away your cat's kittens. You *never* get over it! If you have any friends who are adopted, please tell them that their birth moms are probably thinking about them every day and dreaming about them every night. As a matter of fact, maybe your cat never gets over losing her kittens, either."

"So how did you get Orchid back?" I asked.

"Looking back on it now, the whole thing seems like a miracle," Jasmine said. "I had dropped out of college and was working a crappy waitress job when I ran into my former dance teacher. She said she was opening her own academy and asked me to go into business with her. So I found myself making good money at a job that I loved. And I thought to myself, what would Orchid think of me if she found out later that her birth mother and father both had successful businesses and had given her up for adoption? How do you reconcile something like that?"

"So, long story short," Jasmine continued. "I went to Eddie . . . " She caught herself. "I mean—the father—and I asked him to oppose the adoption—we had never established paternity but he still could claim parental rights—it's a legal technicality that you all should know about. And the adoptive family was forced to give her back to me."

"Geez," I said. "That must have been tough! Did you have a relationship with the adopting family?"

"Yes." Jasmine grew pensive. "That was the hardest part. I really liked them. They were a loving, deserving couple, and they could not conceive a child of their own. This is in no way a judgment of them." Jasmine paused. "Allison, if you are watching this, you are in my thoughts every day and I hope that you have found a child, by now, to call your own. This was not easy for me. I know you would have been a great mom to Orchid." Jasmine started to choke up. "I know you *are* a great mom. I picked you myself." Jasmine sobbed. "But this is my baby. Orchid is *my* baby. And I just could not live without her."

I waited a moment to let Jasmine compose herself.

"So," I said. "Bring us up to date. How are you two doing? How are you managing it all?"

"Orchid is now eighteen months old," Jasmine said. "She is walking and talking and we are working on potty training."

"What is it like being a single working mom?" I asked.

"Well, I'm not single anymore," Jasmine said. "We have been living with Tadge—he is the father of one of my dance students—for six months now. His wife died a few years ago and his daughter, Greta, is eleven. Oh, and Greta wanted me to tell you that she is a huge Luci Video fan!" Jasmine grabbed Orchid's chubby hand and waved it at the camera. "Orchid, say, 'Hi, Greta!'"

Orchid giggled and babbled.

"You let Greta watch my show?" I was astonished.

"Your show is all about girl power, am I right?" Jasmine said. "Taking back our bodies, taking back our stories. I work with a lot of young girls at my dance academy and I try to be a mentor and a role model to all of them. Puberty hits so early these days, sometimes as young as the age of ten. And all of my dancers are very body-conscious and get a lot of attention from boys. If they can learn from my experience and your experience so they can avoid going through what we went through, you will have done them an enormous service."

"So your story has a happy ending," I said. "Tadge—is that his name? He must be quite a bit older than you?"

"You know, it's funny," Jasmine said. "I hadn't

dated in a couple of years before I had Orchid and I was really depressed when I came back home without her. Tadge just came into my life one day and he made everything possible. He helped me get Orchid back." She paused. "Tadge, I love you."

Jasmine's video got four million views.

Nineteen

"**W**ELCOME TO *REAL TEEN MOMS* BROUGHT TO YOU by Luci Video," I said into the camera. "Yay, videos!"

"Our guest today is Candace Parker," I checked my notes on my iPad. "Candace was a senior at a prep school in New Hampshire and was having unprotected sex with her boyfriend when she got pregnant. She has a cute baby boy, named Matteo. That is an interesting name. How did you pick it?"

"Hi," Candace smiled into her web cam. "Hi everyone! This is Matty." She held her son up to the camera.

"How old is Matty?" I asked.

"He is sixteen months old, now," Candace said. "And the thing about babies—each day is a little easier than the day before. Every day he learns something new and is a little more independent. Like now, he is eating solid foods and can feed himself, sort of. Most of the food gets into his mouth. A lot of it ends up on the kitchen floor." Candace laughed.

"Wait. You went to St. Paul's in New Hampshire, right?" I asked. "You weren't a 'Senior Salute' victim, were you?"

Candace snorted. "God, no! That's what they call it when the senior boys prey on freshman girls. Danilo and I were both seniors. We dated for a few months."

"So when you found out that you were pregnant, you never considered abortion as an option?" I asked.

"Not really," Candace said. "My mom did, for sure! She wanted me to get an abortion. But I could already feel him moving inside of me and

I loved my little Squirt—that's what I was calling him at the time. I couldn't imagine killing him—it just felt so wrong. Then, my mom took me to an adoption agency but luckily, because the father is from Italy, they didn't want to take the case—too messy, legally. So by default, I got to keep my baby. Yay!"

"So, bring us up to date," I said. "Where are you living? Are you in school?"

Candace frowned. "I am still living at home. I am taking classes at UMass Boston and I am working as a hostess in a restaurant downtown."

"What are you studying?" I asked.

"I am pre-med," Candace said. "My goal is to go to medical school and become an OB-GYN and work exclusively with pregnant teens. Isn't that a cool idea? Wouldn't every pregnant teen out there wish there was a specialist in their town?"

"That is very cool," I said. "How are you managing all of this? Who takes care of Matty?"

"On the days when I have class, I take him with

me," Candace said. "There is a daycare center on campus. On the nights when I have to work, Julia watches him. Julia is our housekeeper."

"That sounds exhausting. Does your mom help out?" I asked.

Candace twisted her mouth into a grimace. "No," she said. "My mom has never been terribly supportive. She wanted me to abort Matty, remember?"

"What about dating?" I asked.

Candace snorted. "Dating? Who would want to date a girl with a baby? Sure, guys hit on me at work sometimes—guys at the bar. But when I tell them I have a kid, they lose interest right away."

"So what's the hardest thing about being a teen mom?" I asked.

Candace looked down as she thought about it; maybe she was looking at Matty. Then she looked back into the camera. "The hardest thing is that I don't have any friends." Her eyes welled up. "All of my friends are away at school. I follow them on

Facebook but they never call me anymore. Nobody ever invites me to hang out."

"What about meeting people at school?" I asked.

"UMass is a commuter school," Candace said. "There isn't any social scene. Just people coming and going, nobody seems too interested in getting to know anyone else. And all of the moms at day-care are way older than me."

"You sound really lonely," I said.

Candace's face brightened. "I've got Matty," she said. She held him up to the camera again. She rubbed her face in his tummy. "Don't I baby? I got you, right?"

"What about your boyfriend? Matty's daddy?" I asked.

Candace frowned again. "He's not my boy-friend. He probably never really was my boyfriend. We broke up before I even knew I was pregnant."

"Does he know about Matty?" I asked. "Is he in the picture?"

"Yeah, he knows," Candace said. "His family

is paying child support. But no, he is not in the picture. He doesn't want to have anything to do with us. Maybe some day, when Matty is older, they might have a relationship. That could happen, right?" She sounded uncertain.

"Any regrets?" I asked.

"About Matty?" Candace replied. She looked away from the camera and sighed. "He won't ever see this, will he? Because I love my baby so much." She looked back into the camera and said, "But I wish I . . . I wish I could travel back in time and make some different choices."

"Like what?" I asked.

"I never really felt like I fit in at prep school," she said. "I guess I didn't really try that hard. I had a pretty snarky attitude back then. But if I had never gone there, I would never have met Danilo and I would never have gotten pregnant and I would be at Princeton now. Did you know that I was accepted into Princeton before all of this happened? Looking back on it, I wish I had gone to Brookline High with all of my middle school friends. I am realizing now how important it is to have friends and how hard it is to make friends when you are not in school. I see my sister and all of her friends getting ready to go off to college and I wish that was me doing that. I wish I could have a do-over."

Wow, this is so different from the Jasmine episode. Candace's story was really sad. *Sadder than mine, even.*

"You seem really sad," I said.

"The last time I can remember being happy was in middle school. I was a fat kid but I was a good singer. I had a singing role in the school musical. I know it sounds crazy but my dream was to be a Broadway actress. Dumb, huh?"

"Did you watch the Jasmine episode of *Real Teen Moms*?" I asked.

"I did," Candace said. "Isn't she awesome?"

"She is," I said. "But what struck me is how dance has played such a big part in her finding happiness. What if you got involved with a community theater group? You could meet new people and make friends?"

Candace's face fell. "Maybe when Matty is a little older," she said. "Right now, it's all I can do to keep up with school and work and taking care of him. Don't get me wrong, I know how lucky I am to be able to live at home and have my dad paying my tuition and then there's Julia, our housekeeper—she is awesome! She helps me with Matty. There is no way I could afford to pay for rent and childcare and tuition on my own. I know a lot of girls in my situation don't have it as easy as me. But my parents have made it clear that they don't want to have anything do to with supporting Matty. He is my responsibility. The phrase my mom uses a lot is: 'you made your bed, now lie in it.'"

"Wow, that's harsh," I said. "But hey! We could be friends. Besides on Facebook, I mean. Friends in real life."

Candace grinned. "That would be nice. Thank you."

"And think of all the girls watching this video," I said. "They could be your friends, too. You could wear a body cam and we could stream you on periscope. All of my viewers could follow you all day long."

"Oh my God," Candace gasped. "That would be so funny! Do you have any idea the amount of hostility that a stroller generates on a crowded sidewalk or on a bus? We could put a baby cam on Matty and view the world through his eyes!"

Candace's video got two million views. But the best part is that she got thirty thousand friend requests on Facebook.

Twenty

"**W**ELCOME TO *REAL TEEN MOMS* BROUGHT TO YOU by Luci Video," I said into the camera. "Yay, videos!"

"Today we'll be talking to Shawna Black, live from our studio in Oakland, California." I checked my notes on my iPad. "Shawna was seventeen and a senior in high school when she got pregnant the first time she had sex with her boyfriend, Philippe. She has a beautiful baby boy named Jack who is fifteen months old, am I right? Welcome Shawna and Jack!"

"That's right!" Shawna beamed into the web cam. "Here's Jack! He's fifteen months old and I haven't killed him yet!" She held Jack up to the camera. His faced was smeared with jelly. "Sorry! He was in the middle of eating his breakfast. It's still early out here in California."

I laughed. "What do you mean, you haven't killed him yet?"

"You know the crazy thing about babies?" Shawna said. "Is that they are basically always doing something that could kill them. Like falling down stairs or banging their head on the coffee table or climbing onto a hot stove or wandering into the street or crawling into a swimming pool. I figured out that a mom's main purpose is to simply keep her child alive until he is eighteen or twenty and then hope for the best."

I imagine the sound of studio laughter.

"So your story is a little unique," I said, glancing at my notes. "When you found out you were pregnant, what did your mom say?"

"She wanted me to keep the baby," Shawna said. "She even said she would raise Jack for me."

"How did you feel about that?" I asked.

"Honestly, it kind of freaked me out," Shawna said. "I'm sure you read the *US Weekly* story about Jack Nicholson?"

"No," I said. "What story?"

"Well, basically his grandmother raised him when his mom got pregnant," Shawna said. "But they told him that his grandmother was his mom and his mom was his sister. He didn't know the truth until he was an adult. I was worried that my mom was going to do that to my Jack—tell him that I was his sister."

"That is creepy!" I said.

"Fortunately, that's not what my mom had in mind," Shawna said. "Actually I don't know what she had in mind because she isn't raising Jack. I am. And Philippe's mom helps out."

"But your mom convinced your dad, right?" I said.

"I am pretty sure every girl on this show tells the same story. Her family pressured her to get an abortion and then for one reason or another, she just couldn't go through with it, right? Philippe and his parents and my dad all wanted me to abort Jack. My mom fought back against all of them. Philippe's parents were really pissed. My dad is an attorney and he got them to agree to pay child support."

"So that is why you decided to have the baby?" I asked.

"No, it would not have changed anything. I had already decided to have the baby. But as my mom said to me back then, it takes a village to raise a child and now both of our families have stepped up to support us and make it possible for Philippe and me to stay in college."

"Is Philippe's family still pissed?" I asked.

"His dad is pissed about the money, yeah," Shawna said.

"Are you living with Philippe?" I asked.

"No, but we are planning to get married!" Shawna exclaimed. "He lives at home with his parents and I live with my parents but we are still together."

"When are you planning to get married?" I asked.

"I don't know—when we finish college and get jobs and make enough money to get our own place," Shawna said. "Jack will probably be ten years old by then. Just kidding."

"What is the hardest thing about being a teen mom?" I asked.

"I was just watching the Candace episode," Shawna said. "And it's what she said. I have no friends. The friends I had in high school, and all the kids at Berkeley—all they want to do is go to concerts and get high and party all night. I can't relate to them. They don't want to go to the playground with Jack and me. And all the other moms at the playground are like ancient—like thirty-something. And the people at the pediatrician's office are the worst. Everyone there treats me like I must be incompetent. By the time my friends get around to having babies, Jack will be so much older than their kids. Who will he play with? Will the other moms in kindergarten want to schedule play dates with Jack? What if he has no friends?"

"Do you think you will want to have more kids?" I asked.

"I sure hope so," Shawna said. "I am an only child and Philippe is an only child. We don't want Jack to be an only child. But we're not planning on having another baby until after we get married. That will be years from now. I'm only going to school part-time—like Candace."

"Why is that?" I asked.

"I tried going full-time and I couldn't keep up with the work," Shawna said. "I was so tired all of the time that I kept falling asleep when I was supposed to be doing my homework. Things got a little better when Jack started sleeping through the night. I am registered for a full course-load in the fall. We'll see how it goes."

"And what about your mom?" I asked. "Does she help with Jack?"

"No!" Shawna said. "That was all bullshit. My mom works full-time. She's a professor at Berkeley. She has never been around to help. Philippe's mom helps out a lot, though. She watches Jack two to three nights a week. My mom watches him every once in a while so Philippe and I can have a date night."

"What kind of a dad is Philippe?" I asked.

Shawna frowned and pursed her lips. "Philippe is just a kid," she said. "He is good for driving Jack back and forth between our houses, but when it comes to taking responsibility for feeding him, bathing him, putting him to sleep, Philippe is kind of useless. I watched the Jasmine episode and I think she got the formula right. It's okay to be a teen mom, if your partner is an adult dad. But a teen dad? Please! That should be your next vlog series: *Real Teen Dads*. What a joke! Put a body cam on a teen dad—that would be good for a laugh. Now *that* baby might not survive as long."

"It would be like Survivor: Baby Edition!" I said.

Shawna guffawed. "That's perfect!"

"Any regrets?" I asked.

"Sure!" Shawna said. "I wish the condom had worked. I wish I had been on the pill. I have an IUD now—we are not taking any more chances. We love Jack but like Philippe said to me—the plan was to finish college, get married, and have kids. Oops, we got things a little bit out of order."

"Any advice for our audience?" I asked.

"Use birth control!" Shawna shook her finger at the web cam. "Two forms of birth control at all times!"

Twenty One

"WELCOME TO *REAL TEEN MOMS* BROUGHT TO YOU by Luci Video," I said into the camera. "Yay, videos!"

"Live from St. Louis, Missouri, it's Isabella Moran." I checked my notes on my iPad. "Izzy was eighteen when her husband, Carlos, was killed in Afghanistan and she was already pregnant with their son, George. How old is George, now?" I asked.

Izzy waived at the web cam. "Hi," she shouted.

"You don't need to shout," I said. "We can hear you just fine."

"What?" Izzy shouted.

"Izzy, turn up the volume on your computer," I said. I kicked myself for forgetting to do a sound check with Izzy before we started streaming. "Test, test, test," I repeated as Izzy poked at her keyboard.

"Okay," she said. "I can hear you now."

"Great!" I said. "Let's start over. Can we see George? How old is he?"

Izzy bent over to pick up George and sat him on her lap facing the webcam. "Here he is. George is fourteen months."

"So your story is quite a bit different," I said. "You were already married when you got pregnant?"

"Well, not exactly," Izzy said. "We were engaged but I was already pregnant before we got married. My parents were *not* happy."

"About the pregnancy?" I asked.

"About the wedding," she said. "My parents wanted me to go to college. They weren't happy when Carlos asked me to marry him. They couldn't figure out why we had to get married if I wasn't already pregnant—and I wasn't at the time. They were worried that I wouldn't finish college."

"And?" I asked.

"They were right, of course," Izzy said. "Carlos had already enlisted and he wanted to get married before he was deployed. It was a real nice wedding and we had a honeymoon in New Orleans right before he left. But I got pregnant right away and it has been real hard, just George and me. So, no, I am not in school. I work as a hairdresser."

"What about your parents?" I asked. "Are you living with them?"

"My mom kicked me out right after the wedding and I moved in with Carlos's parents," Izzy said. "His family was really good to me. But then his mom died of cancer right before Carlos died and I felt funny living there. I knew I needed to move out if I was going to get on with my life."

"I'm sorry about Carlos," I said. "Losing him in the war—that must have been awful."

"Yeah," Izzy said. "I feel like we really never got a chance to be married, play house together, you know? I hate this awful war."

"And he never met his son, right?" I asked.

"No, Carlos just saw George as my baby bump on Skype," Izzy said. "But he looks just like his dad. We always say that George is going to grow up to be a senator. That would be so awesome! But he is not allowed to join the Army. No way, no how!"

"So Carlos has been gone for more than a year," I said. "What about dating? Are you dating?"

Izzy stood up, walked over to the playpen and set George down. When she came back to the web cam, her expression was fierce.

"So this is about to get real," she said. "Girls, and I mean all you girls out there who watch Luci Video, listen to me. Nobody is ever going to love your baby the way you do. It's just like what Candace said; nobody wanted to date her once they found out that she had a kid. I didn't have that problem but George was not Pete's kid."

"Who is Pete?" I asked.

"Pete is a guy I knew in high school," Izzy said. "He was really more of Carlos's friend. We ran into each other right before Carlos died and then when I coincidentally went into labor in his car, he took me to the hospital."

"You went into labor in Pete's car?" I asked. "Is that what you said?"

"Yeah, we were just friends then but I ran into him again last year, at work. We hooked up a few months ago and moved in together. That sounds like a happy ending, right? Your husband is killed in a war and then an old friend from high school shows up and wants to date you. Sounds perfect, right?"

"So what went wrong?" I asked.

"Like I said, George was not Pete's kid. Your

guy may say he loves you and that your kid is just part of the package. But it is not true. Babies can be annoying. They cry, they are messy, and they always need your attention. Everything George did annoyed Pete and we fought about it. A lot! And Pete was mean to George, I mean like scary-ass mean. I mean like, murderous mean."

"Did Pete ever hurt George?" I asked.

"Pete hit me all the time," Izzy said. "I didn't know what to do. I didn't think I could escape. I didn't know where to go. I don't make that much money and even with Carlos's military benefits, it's still hard balancing everything: rent and food and gas and childcare—you get the picture. But when I saw how scared George was, I knew I had to get him the hell out of there."

"That is really scary," I said.

"Yeah, you hear about this shit all of the time—domestic violence," Izzy said. "But then when it happens to you, you can't believe it's happening. I mean, why would a man ever need to hit a woman?"

"Why do they?" I asked.

"I've had a lot of therapy," Izzy said. "And what I learned is that the biggest misconception about these guys is that they have 'anger management' issues. They don't. They don't blow up at work or at the driver who cuts into their lane. Instead they have an overwhelming need to control their girlfriend—how she dresses, where she goes, and whom she talks to. That's why, before they actually start using physical violence to stay in control, they are often constantly phoning and text-messaging her so that they know exactly what she is doing at all times. They most likely grew up in a home where there was violence. I know Pete did. His dad hit his mom. They think it's okay."

Izzy pointed her finger at the camera. "It's not," she said. "It's not okay!"

"And when you say you didn't know where to go—your mom wouldn't take you in?" I asked.

"No, that was never an option," Izzy said. "My mom was mean to George too, in other ways. She is a drunk. This poor little boy! None of this is his doing. I brought him into this world. Carlos and me, I mean. We were so much in love, everything felt so right. Until everything went so wrong."

"So what now?" I asked.

"We are living in my cousin's basement," Izzy said. "And I am working in her salon. It's not a bad setup, at least until I can save up and find us a place of our own."

"What about Carlos's family?" I asked. "Couldn't you move back in with them?"

"It's just Carlos's dad and his brothers now," Izzy said. "I don't think they ever really forgave me for moving in with Pete. Like I was desecrating Carlos's memory or some bullshit like that. I guess they thought I should be the lonely widow my whole life. Well, I probably will be now, right?"

"Any advice for our audience?" I asked.

Izzy's expression looked wise beyond her years. "Stay in school!" she shouted. "Go to college! There's plenty of time to have babies once you are done with school."

Twenty Two

"**W**ELCOME TO *REAL TEEN MOMS* BROUGHT TO YOU by Luci Video," I said into the camera. "Yay, videos!"

"Joining us today from Ft. Pierce, Florida is Aleecia Rivera." I scanned through the notes on my iPad. "Aleecia was fifteen when the condom broke on prom night. She has a sweet little baby girl, named Mia. How old is Mia now?"

Aleecia sat nervously in front of her web cam holding Mia in her lap. She was still carrying probably an extra ninety pounds of baby weight and looked much older than sixteen.

"Hello?" Aleecia's voice wavered. "This is Mia." She held her up. "She is thirteen months old."

"So what about the baby-daddy?" I asked. "What happened to him?

"Kyle?" Aleecia said. "He is in Tallahassee. He wants to be a good daddy but we are not together anymore."

"Tell us your story," I coaxed.

"Um, yeah—well, like you said," Aleecia said. "Kyle was a senior and he came into my work one day—I work as a cashier at Big Lots. He was the captain of the football team and I was so excited that he knew my name! I couldn't believe it! And then he asked me out; we used to take long walks on the beach. And then he came to my church several times—I sing in the choir you know? And then he invited me to his prom and I was so excited! I didn't know that he had rented a room at a motel where the after-parties were being held. But I drank too much—I got pretty drunk that night. I think I passed out on the bed. I really don't remember too much about that night. Kyle told me later that the condom had fallen apart."

"Then what happened?" I asked.

"My momma was mad as hell," Aleecia said. "She grounded me and then when I found out that I was pregnant, she drove me to an abortion clinic in Orlando. There were protesters and everything."

"But you decided to keep the baby?" I asked.

"I loved Kyle and he loved me," Aleecia said. "It just didn't feel right to kill our baby. And Kyle said he wanted to marry me."

"What did your mother think about that?" I asked.

"Well, you know my mama got pregnant when she was a teenager and she kept me," Aleecia said. "It's not what she wanted for me, obviously, but we are happy, the three of us."

"Kyle wanted to marry you?" I asked. "What happened?"

"He wanted to do the right thing. He never knew his daddy and he wanted our baby to have a daddy. And then his mom threw him out so he and his little brother moved into my mom's garage for a while. He was going to fix it up like a little guest cottage for the three of us. And then we were going to move to Nashville and take his little brother and sister with us."

"But that didn't happen?" I prodded.

"Well, then he got recruited to play football for Florida State," Aleecia said. "So, of course, he couldn't pass up that opportunity. But it wasn't long after he left that I stopped hearing from him as much. He seemed to get real preoccupied, you know, with college and football and cheerleaders and whatnot."

Aleecia paused and leaned down to kiss Mia's head.

"You know that really surprised me. I thought he would come home every weekend. But it is a long drive—I know that. And he had his little brother with him. Kyle didn't come from a stable home situation. He had to look out for his little brother."

"Are you still in school?" I asked.

"Yeah, I am a junior now" Aleecia said. "I stayed in school the whole time. My school has a special program for the preggos. I guess all schools have that these days? And my church choir let me back in after Mia was born. They said they couldn't have a pregnant teen singing in the choir but they seem to be okay with me now. Although I think Father Rick had something to do with that."

"Who is Father Rick?" I asked.

"He is my Pastor," Aleecia said. "He is my spiritual advisor. He was there at Mia's birth and he is like a father to us both."

"Was Kyle there for Mia's birth?" I asked.

"No," Aleecia said, sadly. "He was away at school."

"So how are you managing everything—being in high school and being a mom?" I asked.

"My mom works twelve-hour shifts as a

home-aide taking care of old ladies but I have lots of family around," Aleecia said. "Aunts and cousins. I drop Mia off with my cousin who looks after three other little kids. It's not what I thought we would be doing but it's okay. Mia is happy. I can finish school. It's all good."

"What is the hardest thing about being a teen mom?" I asked.

"Candace," Aleecia said into the web cam. "I hope you are watching this. I am sorry that you don't have any friends—I friended you on Facebook. Maybe it's the difference between Boston and Florida, but I have *lots* of teen mom friends. I have a whole cohort at my high school. And some in my church group and one where I work—at Big Lots. We get together with the kids. I have a baby pool in my backyard and the girls bring their kids over. Mia loves the water."

"So what is the hardest thing?" I repeated.

"Well, money is tight, that is for sure. I would not be here if it weren't for my mom. I pitch in with the household expenses, but there is no way I could be out on my own. Even after I graduate high school, I will probably be living at home for years, decades, maybe." Aleecia laughed.

"Kids are real expensive—they grow out of their clothes every six weeks or so! But I also think it's kind of like what Izzy said. I don't know that I will ever find a husband—someone who would love my daughter, Mia, and me equally. I know Father Rick loves us and maybe someday we will get married."

"Father Rick wants to marry you?" I asked. I thought about my interview with Amanda and Father William. "Has he tried to kiss you or anything?"

"Father Rick?" Aleecia snorted. "Hell, no! He's a holy man. You are thinking of Father William. I googled *Father William* after I watched Amanda's video. I think they arrested him."

Oh shit! They arrested Father William?

"Any advice for our audience?" I asked.

Aleecia's expression was solemn. "Believe in the Lord. And don't trust condoms."

"Bless you, Aleecia," I said. "I hope you find happiness. You can still move to Nashville and pursue the Gospel singing thing, you know."

"I know. But first I need to finish high school and lose about a hundred pounds."

Aleecia's video got three million views.

Twenty Three

WELL, THAT IS MY STORY. **A**ND THE REST AS THEY SAY, is history. After the first *Real Teen Moms* series concluded, my inbox overflowed with requests from girls all over the country wanting to be on my show. I also had a few dozen inquiries about the *Real Teen Dad* series as well as a couple for *Survivor: Baby Edition* although I was hoping those folks were joking.

My mom didn't know about any of this, of course. She thought I was just upstairs in my room doing my homework. And my dad had a girlfriend by then so I didn't see much of him anymore.

I was just finishing up my sophomore year of

high school when Netflix called. Somehow my promiscuous lifestyle and unwanted pregnancy had given birth (sorry for the pun) to a whole new media empire. I was offered a Netflix original series plus a line of books, graphic novels, and teen maternity clothing. I had become a role model for girls everywhere. My logo included the phrases: "Love Yourself" and "Don't Trust Boys."